# APOCALYPSE THE BEGINNING

## THE POWER OF TWELVE BOOK ONE

MIRANDA MARTIN

# CONTENTS

Apocalypse the Beginning © 2019-2020 Miranda Martin

Previously published as Divine Gift

# PROLOGUE

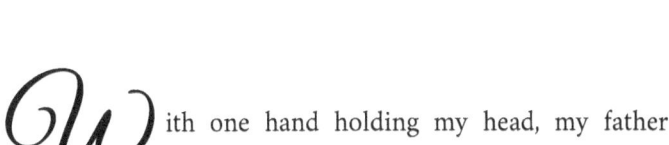

*W*ith one hand holding my head, my father sweeps me off my feet and into his arms, crushing me against his chest. "Aviella, close your eyes."

It's hard to breathe with my face pressed against the warm, damp cotton of his shirt. His smell is everywhere. Verbena, musk, and a scent that's just him.

"It's okay, we're fine," he repeats over and over.

I squish my eyes closed and clench my fist, trying to hold on to my blue balloon. Something explodes close to us. It's so loud my ears start to ring and a rush of hot air passes over us.

I scream, a muffled cry buried in my daddy's shoulder.

"Breathe baby, breathe," he reassures me. "Mommy is watching over us, we'll be fine," he says.

He always says things like that. 'Mommy is watching over us'. It's his thing, but the older I get the less it matters. I've never known my mom. She's a myth to me. I know I had a mother of course, everyone does, but there's no connection. She gave birth to me and was gone, leaving my father and me alone. It's always been us, just the two of us, and that's fine.

Kids in school ask me about it but I lie. I tell them my mom died when I was born, which isn't true, according to daddy anyway.

She's not dead, she's in heaven, he says. Right, living people don't go to heaven.

Or they didn't, until a full third of the world disappeared.

No one knows what happened, but they left a hell of a mess behind. Months later my school was filled with people claiming the Rapture had come and those who went missing were the chosen who went to heaven.

I don't know and I don't want to. Everything about it makes the noise buzz, deep in my bones, like billions of bees inside of me trying to get out.

I'm bouncing in my father's arms as he runs. Inside my head the noise starts, the ringing in my ears making it louder. The dull roar that precedes *it* happening, the thing inside me that makes bad things happen and hurts people.

No, no, no, hold it down, hold it down, I say over and over in my head. I can't let it go. It will only make things worse. I'm so scared though. There's so much screaming and shouting and more explosions.

I sneak a peek out of one eye, opening it just enough to get a glimpse. We're crouched next to a gray car. Daddy's head swivels back and forth but he doesn't see the man coming up behind us with a crazed look in his eyes; mouth hanging open with drool, hands grasping.

My throat goes dry.

I try to warn my father, but no sound comes. The roaring fills my ears as my heart beats faster. I try so hard but I can't keep *it* inside anymore and the bad thing escapes. My eyes snap open and it explodes.

The man screams, a gargled sound, flying backwards through the air until his cry is cut off, his body slamming against the brick wall of an apartment building thirty feet away. Daddy whirls around, staying crouched and holding me tight. His hand convulses on the back of my head and he gasps seeing the mess I've made.

Tears leak through my clenched eyelids as the buzzing noise recedes. "I'm sorry!"

"It's fine baby, you're fine," he says. "We've got to get home, back to the apartment."

"Okay," I hiccup.

"You have to be a big girl now," he says, pulling me just far enough away to make me look him in the eyes. "You're my special girl. Mommy and I love you so much. Don't ever forget that. You know it right?"

"Yes, Daddy," I reply, tightening back my grip around his neck.

I do too. Something swells in my chest until it hurts. I know how much he loves me.

"If we get separated, get to the apartment," he says.

Something in his voice is scary.

Letting go, I push away from him to stand on my own. His deep blue eyes look sad and his face is serious, the same face he makes when I'm in trouble. The blue balloon tied to my wrist sways in the breeze. Daddy holds my stuffed, white rhino in his left hand, placing his right hand on my cheek.

Why is he so sad? "Daddy?"

He shakes his head, swallowing, then nods. "Yes sweet-pea," he says. "Promise me. Okay? Please, just promise me."

"Yes okay," I force the words past the lump in my throat. "I'm sorry. I tried to hold it down. I didn't mean to let it go."

He glances over his shoulder at the mess I made. When he looks back there's a smile on his face and he shakes his head. "It's fine baby," he says. "It was a bad man. There are going to be more bad men. Bad things. You have to be safe."

Today was supposed to be a special day. The big event in the park was supposed to make things normal again, not weird. Everyone was coming out to celebrate and on top of that it's my birthday, I'm nine years old today. This isn't fair! There were elephants. I wanted to ride one and Daddy said I could, but then the ground shook and everyone was screaming.

The elephants trumpeted and fought against the ties holding them in place. My dad was quick, grabbing me and running before the rest of the crowd panicked. He said something about 'it wasn't supposed to happen yet' but I didn't know what he meant, and the ground had trembled again. It's only gotten worse since.

A line of dark shadow passes across the car and my father's face. Looking up, the sky is not as bright as it was. Something huge is moving across the sun. Daddy is watching it too.

"Is it an eclipse?" I ask.

He swallows so hard I can hear it, then he grabs me by my shoulders. "Sweet-pea," he says, urgency in his voice and grip. "You do what you have to do okay? No matter what happens, you survive. Stay safe but don't let people know what you can do. You're special. You're my little girl and I love you so much."

Gooseflesh ripples across my arms and my spine tightens. "You're scaring me!"

I fling my arms around him and grip his sweat-dampened shirt with all I've got. The darkness becomes so deep the car next to us disappears. Something roars and it's so loud I scream, pressing my face harder into my father's chest. The sound digs into me and it feels like it's in my bones.

*It* comes, rattling my insides, pouring out of me with my shout.

Everything is silent.

Slowly I raise my head from his shoulder, ears still buzzing, and open my eyes. The car we were crouching behind is a dozen feet away on its side. Daddy and I are in a circle of nothing, even the dirt and debris of the street has moved away from us.

My dad blinks, shakes his head and says something. I can't hear his words. His mouth moves but the sound doesn't cut through my ringing ears. His strong hands clamp on either side of my head and he pulls me close, kissing my forehead. Rising from his crouch he takes my hand, looks around, then pulls me along beside him, almost running.

The abandoned street glows red. The sky is dark and where the sun should be is a big, pulsing black spot with blood red lines. It looks like a black eye with bloody veins. My stomach turns over on itself and I think I'm going to vomit. I try to keep up with my father but my stomach clenches. Pulling my hand from his, I stop, bending over and retching. He goes a few steps before turning back.

"I'm sorry," I say, gasping air.

I'm burning hot and sweat is pouring into my eyes as I try to stop my stomach. It hurts so much. The buzzing inside keeps getting louder. It wants to get out but I can't let it. It hurts people.

"It's fine baby girl," Daddy says, pressing cool hands to my cheeks and forehead. He keeps looking around and I can tell he's scared. "We have to move Aviella Marie."

I think I might puke again. He used my whole name. He never uses my whole name, he hardly ever uses my name at all. This is bad. It's so, so bad.

"Okay," I say, gasping in a deep breath.

I will not vomit. I will not vomit.

Dad nods, grabs my hand, and turns, all but running down the sidewalk. The tall buildings blur by as we move.

Fresh rounds of screams drift down the street to us. We're only blocks from home. So close. We'll be safe there.

I focus on my feet. The sidewalk is broken in a lot of places, jagged pieces sticking up make it hard not to trip. It wasn't like this when we left for the celebration.

"Sweet heaven help us," Daddy gasps.

A huge crowd runs down the street heading straight for us. Their eyes are wide and their mouths are open in an endless scream as they push and shove at each other. Three people in the front fall but the crowd doesn't slow, trampling right over them. Dad grabs me, pulling me to his chest as he turns and runs. Watching over his shoulder, the crowd closes in on us. Dad runs fast and my head bounces against his shoulder, jarring me with each step.

We're going the wrong way! Home is behind us, past the mob of crazy people.

A loud, thrumming sound echoes off tall buildings growing louder. Something passes overhead, a shadow in the shadows. I don't see what it is, but the mob stops almost like they're one person. They drop to their knees, covering their heads with their arms and screaming. Daddy's hand pushes my head down as he bends over me, still running.

"Don't look baby, don't look," he huffs, breathless from the effort of running and carrying me.

The screams rise in pitch and I squeeze my eyes shut, listening to him. If there's one thing I know, Daddy's right. He's always right, but my heart hurts as the screams grow louder. *It* buzzes, like it wants to help. But it never helps, all it ever does is get me in trouble or hurt someone.

No, I can't let *it* go. I can't look. Shouldn't look.

I can't help it, really, my eye opens just a little. It's not really my fault. I'm bouncing awfully hard. I gasp, wishing I could have listened.

A glowing man, pure white with feathery wings and

holding a massive, blood-drenched sword hovers over the mob. They're begging before him, lying on the ground and screaming for his mercy. It's an angel. Or it looks like one. Above the angel is a dragon. Huge, wings spreading out further than I can see, moving through the air with an easy grace that something that big shouldn't have.

The buzzing grows louder than the screaming mob's pleas.

"Aviella, no," Daddy says, urgency in his voice.

Sometimes it seems like he knows when I'm about to do something, or *it* is. Swallowing, I fight with everything I have to hold the buzzing in. We turn a corner and once I can't see the angel any longer it fades.

Letting go of the breath I didn't realize I was holding, it hits me. A dragon. Wow, I don't know if that's cool or scary. Or both? Yeah, both.

Suddenly I'm flying through the air, tumbling free of Daddy's arms.

"AVIELLA!"

It's funny because everything is moving slow. Super slow, like a movie. The sidewalk below me cracks open, thrusting up, then I see the sky, black with streaks of red, before I flip back over to see the sidewalk still moving. It's like I'm watching this happen to someone else. Turning over again I find my dad, he's in the air too, almost like he's flying. My dad could be an angel. A real angel, full of God's love. The ground is coming closer and I know this is going to hurt. I close my eyes and wait for the pain.

Time returns to normal as I slam against the sidewalk. White-hot pain wracks my body, too much to understand. Distant screams fill my ears and a gross blood taste is in my mouth. Sliding to a halt, I lie still. It hurts to breathe and my face feels like it's on fire.

I think that's the worst of it though, I can move my arms

and legs. Pushing off the sidewalk to my knees I open my eyes. Blood streaks the concrete and oh my god is it mine? I have to find my dad.

Climbing to my feet, I touch my cheek and wish I hadn't. The sharp pain comes and once more my stomach clenches tight. Okay, don't do that. The air is full of dust and the ground rumbles under my feet again as a loud roar echoes off the buildings.

Probably the dragon. It sounds like what I think a dragon would sound like anyway. I don't know if that makes it a dragon or not. It could be some other monster. Or the angel. Maybe angels sound like roaring dragons.

Pay attention Aviella. I can't let myself be distracted. I have to find my dad.

"Daddy?" I call, waving my hand to try and clear the dust from the air.

The rumbling in the ground grows stronger. The vibration is traveling up my legs, shaking my chest. More dust rises into the air. The rows of buildings next to me puff out blasts of reddish brown dirt, making it impossible to see. Coughing, I stumble forward, eyes closed, trying to get away from it. I avoid tripping over a broken piece of the sidewalk and finally get clear of the dust cloud. Stepping out and opening my eyes fully, the crazy crowd is running right at me. They're scarily silent. All of them have their mouths open like they're screaming but there's no sound. Their eyes are so wide I can see the whites and their faces are all almost the same color.

A few feet in front of me is my white rhino but there's no sign of my dad. I look from the rhino to the crowd. Another roar echoes around me, bouncing off the walls of the buildings on either side.

Another crack tears the street as the ground rumbles. The crowd tries to part around it but something huge, like a giant red-pink tentacle, reaches out and sweeps a bunch of them into the chasm. Now they scream, the sounds of their voices fading as they fall to whatever fate awaits them.

I'm frozen in place, too scared to move. I need my Daddy.

My eyes fall on my white rhino. Dingy with dirt, lying on the broken sidewalk, one glass eye staring back at me like to say, why are you leaving me here? Pushing hard, my foot moves forward. A little at first then I break through my fear. The crowd is coming closer. Still silent, which is somehow scarier than if they were screaming. Kneeling, I grab the toy, pausing to look around once, hoping to see my dad. On the other side of a parked car a foot catches my attention. That's his shoe!

"Daddy!" I yell, jumping to my feet and running, hope full in my chest.

That horrible tentacle thing swings out again and sweeps another chunk of the crowd to their doom. The rest of them continue racing forward, less than a hundred feet away. Running around the car I skid to a halt. The body lying there isn't my dad. My heart sinks as hope dies away.

"AVIELLA!" Dad's voice cries.

Turning quickly, I spot him. He's on the far side of the street, waving his arms wildly.

"Daddy!" I scream, moving forward but the ground rumbles then bucks underneath me.

The street rips apart just in front of my feet. Backpedaling, heart pounding in my chest, I gasp air as I struggle to not fall into the widening opening. It stops growing at last, but now there's a huge gap separating me and my dad. Moving carefully toward the edge, I look down and my head spins. It's deeper than I can see.

"Aviella."

He's on the other side of the chasm.

"Daddy," I say, chills running along my arms and legs. "It's too far."

"I know baby," he says. "I know, get to the house. Okay? Remember, heaven is watching over you sweet-pea."

He looks to his right. The crowd has split to either side of the break in the street and they're close, too close, they're almost on us.

"Run Aviella!" he yells. "I'll meet you there, go!"

My legs move before I can think, responding to his command like they're his legs instead of mine. I clutch the rhino to my chest, holding it tight. A bright light flashes in the sky followed by more screaming. Closing my eyes tight, I run blindly, unable to look. I don't want to know.

*It* buzzes through my bones, making my skin crawl and itch. It hasn't felt like this before.

An explosion happens somewhere close and I look. I don't want to but I do. The dragon is passing overhead, making the buzzing inside me louder. Three angels follow in its wake, brightly glowing swords dripping with blood.

I turn a corner, cut over three blocks, then turn again heading back towards home. I don't stop running. The look on my father's face was enough. I have to get home. He'll be there waiting for me. This street is mostly empty. A few crying people huddle next to steps or behind cars. I stay far away from them, who knows if they would turn on me if I got too close.

The scent of the water says I'm close. Dad insisted our home be close to the water. We have to have multiple routes out of the city, he says. Never let yourself get backed into a corner. Don't stay anywhere you can't get out of at least three ways.

My chest and legs hurt, I've got to stop running so I slide up next to the closest building. Leaning against the cool brick I take a moment to rest. The buzz in my bones is low, almost gone. Maybe that means there's nothing bad close. I hope. Taking a deep breath I hold it and count to ten then let it out slowly. I do it three more times, like dad taught me, and I feel a little better. I make my way to the edge of the building and look around the corner. Home is two blocks that way then another corner. Please, please be clear, I pray.

*It* buzzes louder in my ears when I catch sight of the angel. It's floating three feet over the street, staring the other direction. I pull back around the corner. What do I do now? I have to get past that stupid thing.

"Hey, you," someone shouts.

I risk looking around the corner again. A young boy stands in the middle of the street with a rock in his hand. He has jet black hair and from here his eyes look like emeralds. He waves his hand at the angel, shouting.

"Yeah, you, fly boy!" he yells, brandishing the rock like it's a mighty weapon.

He looks past the angel and I swear our eyes meet across the distance. It buzzes an entirely different tone than ever before. Butterflies dance in my stomach. The dark-haired boy looks back at the angel who's still ignoring him. He throws the stone, beaming it right upside the angel's head. The angel looks down at the rock then back up. The boy smiles, the biggest, goofiest grin I've ever seen.

"That's right," my inadvertent savior mocks the angel. "Come get this."

He turns and runs, fast. Too fast for a boy. I don't know how he does it but right now it doesn't matter because it works. The angel takes off after him, leaving my path home clear. Not wasting time, I run down the street and skid my way around the corner. Everything looks like a scene out of a war movie. Buildings are crumbling, jagged chasms ruin the streets and the sidewalks are shattered. Burning cars lie on their sides.

I run past it all. Dad will be at home waiting for me, worried. I can't keep him waiting.

Leaping over a broken piece of sidewalk, I skid to a stop just past the stairs down to our basement apartment. The soft ringing of our wind chime calls to me as I scramble back and go down the steps two at a time. Pausing, I look around to see if anyone or anything is watching. Lying down on the sidewalk, I crawl up the steps and peek over the edge, carefully studying everything around me, just like Daddy taught me.

Satisfied nothing is paying me any mind, I slide back down the steps on my butt and look up at the wind chime. It's a rock shaped like a diamond with copper pipes dangling below it, sounding in the soft breeze. I reach up but can't get a hold of it. Grabbing one of the two chairs on the other side of the door I drag it over and climb up to the chime. Gripping it in both hands I twist and it opens, revealing a key which I take, slip into my pocket, then put the chime back together.

I put the chair back where it was so it doesn't draw attention. The key turns smoothly in the lock and the door swings open revealing cool darkness.

"Daddy?" I ask. Silence greets me. A knot clenches my stomach. "Daddy?"

Flipping the light switch nothing happens. Okay. He's not here yet. That just means I beat him home. That's all. It's okay, nothing wrong at all.

Closing and locking the door behind me, I bite my lower lip. I don't know what to do now. I plop down on the couch and clutch my white rhino to my chest. A yawn comes out of nowhere making my eyes water. I blink several times, but another comes then another. The dim light coming through the window is growing dimmer and I can't fight it any longer.

Feeling heavy, I get off the couch and walk down the hall to our bedrooms. I pause at the door to mine, looking in at my bed, covered with stuffed animals. No, it's not what I want. I go to the next door and into my father's room. Crawling up onto his bed, I pull the blankets up over my head, surrounding myself with the smell of him.

He'll be here soon. Everything will be fine. He's okay. I think the words over and over until sleep claims me.

I WAKE WITH A START, SITTING STRAIGHT UP IN BED AND throwing the blankets off.

"Daddy?" I call out, heart pounding in my chest.

He should be here. I don't know how long I slept but it must have been long enough for him to make it home. Silence. Straining my ears, I trace every hint of sound, expecting it to be him, but nothing.

In a few minutes my stomach rumbles. Right. I should eat. What do I eat? He always made my food for me. I don't know how to fix anything.

Dropping out of his bed, I rest my hand on his pillow. Come home daddy. I need you.

Nodding I turn and go to the kitchen. Opening each cabinet, then the fridge, I look over all the food on hand. I decide to tray and put two pieces of bread in the toaster. I push the lever down but it pops back up. I know this is how it works so I try again.

"Why aren't you working?" I ask the machine, hoping it might tell me.

Why not? There are weirder things outside my front door. It doesn't, of course. That would be helpful.

"Ugh, of course, there's no electricity," I answer myself.

I pull the bread out and place it on a plate then I

remember the camping stove. I get it out of the closet and set it up, like he showed me. Then I get a pan and pour in some oats and water to boil. While that heats up I spread jelly on the bread in a thick layer. I don't like plain oats, so I dig into the cabinet looking for flavor. Ah! Cinnamon, that's good. Holding the jar over the pot I shake it then a big glump of it plops out into the pot.

"Too much Avi," I admonish myself.

Back into the cabinets I find a container of sugar and figuring why not, I put about the same amount of sugar in as there is cinnamon. Once its boiled for a while I put it into a bowl and set that on the plate next to my bread. Daddy says to always eat a balanced meal. Out of the cabinet I find Mr. Gummi Vitamins and I put five of them on the plate and get out some orange Nutri-aid which I stir into a glass of water. Good, this is everything I should need for breakfast.

Sitting it all on the table I eat, slowly chewing and watching the front door. Any minute now. He's going to walk in any minute.

The minutes become an hour and nothing happens. There are sounds outside. Scary sounds. A tightness grips my chest making it hard to breathe. A tear slips out and down my cheek and I wipe it away. No. I'm not going to cry. Dragging a chair across the floor I set it by the window but it's too high for me to see out. Hmm. Setting my white rhino to one side I grab hold of the table in the dining room and drag. It scrapes loudly across the floor. It takes all I've got to get it under the window, but I make it. Breathing heavily, I lean against it until my muscles stop quivering.

Grabbing the chair, I lift it onto the table and slide it next to the wall then I put my rhino on the table before climbing up. Sitting in the chair I can now see out the high-set window, over the outside wall into the street. A few people are running around in circles like they're lost. Two of them run into each other and then they start fighting. My stomach clenches tight and I crouch down until I'm barely peeking out. I don't want to be seen by the crazy people.

Leaning my head against the cool stone of the outer wall I pass out.

The wall rattles, bouncing my head off it as something explodes nearby. Screaming, I drop my stuffed toy and grab the chair with both hands. My throat hurts I scream so long but I can't stop. Why isn't he here?

Once the house stops rumbling I'm finally able to stop screaming. The tears take a while longer but eventually there doesn't seem to be any of those left either.

I climb down from the chair, look at the kitchen and think about food but even thinking about it makes me nauseous.

Another day passes as I sit, waiting.

Crawling out of his bed, my feet hit the cold floor.

"Day three Aviella, you know what he said to do," I say to myself.

Three days is the limit. We don't wait more than three days. He'll find me, eventually. We prepared for this whether I want to do it or not. An empty feeling consumes my chest and I sob once but I'm out of tears. I spent them all yesterday. Today is it. Survival is on me now. I make myself breakfast, setting my white rhino across the table where daddy would be, if he was here. Finishing my food, I look at it, staring at me with its glass eyes and I sigh. I put my dishes away then pick up the rhino and go to my bedroom.

It's in here somewhere. That nice lady from Protective Services gave it to me after her last checkup. Digging through my stuffed animals I find the fluffy teddy bear she gave me. Turning it upside down the number is there. Dad told me to call them if I ever got lost. He'd be able to find me if I was with them.

Running my finger over the phone number, a tear falls on it. Biting my lip, I go to the closet and dig out the special phone he keeps there. It turns on, but I don't feel any sense of relief. Hands shaking, I put the number in and listen to the line ringing.

This is it. The end of the world as I know it.

# CHAPTER ONE

*T*he air in Matron Bella's office is oppressive. I think it's something she cultivates. Like she's not imposing enough on her own.

Matron Bella is the headmistress of the orphanage. Her sharp features are accented by gray hair at her temples and stormy blue eyes. When she fixes you with her gaze, it's like your soul is being laid bare.

She moves papers around on her desk, not looking at me. Meticulously organizing them like they aren't already in perfect order. She clears her throat, shifts some more papers, then clears her throat again. The hard chair is hurting my butt.

It's part of her plan. You're not supposed to be comfortable when confronting her.

"Aviella," she says, still not looking up.

"Yes Matron?" I ask, attempting to sound innocent.

I'm not, I never am, and she damn well knows it. She reaches to her left and takes a very thick folder off the stack. She holds it by the edges with an air of distaste like she's worried the contents might infect her. Setting it down, she gingerly takes one corner then pulls the folder open. She stares at the first page with an intensity that makes my guts churn. I know it's my file, of course. I'm sure none of the others have one as thick as mine. I'm special that way. Go me.

"Aviella," she repeats, shaking her head like she's reading the saddest story of all time.

Maybe she's. My life's been pretty shit so far.

"Yes Matron?" I ask again out of a sense of duty more than any interest in carrying on a conversation.

She looks up, hitting me with those piercing eyes. I want to look away but I can't. Deep inside *it* buzzes in response, like it's rising to the challenge of her gaze. Cold sweat breaks out on my forehead and back. No, no, no, can't let that go. I struggle to control it, can't let it get away. The buzzing is in my bones and I swear it's like she can see it even though I know she can't.

"You've been with us for," she glances down at the folder, thankfully, and *it* drops away. "Ten years."

"Yes Matron," I say, trying to be agreeable.

We both know how long I've been here. I've spent enough time in her office that my name should be engraved on this flat, hard chair.

"You have... no friends," she says, reading from my file. "No strong connections, display a level of distrust of anyone and everyone, including teachers..."

She trails off like these aren't all things that she and I have already discussed to death. I know, I know, I suck. Can I go now?

Butterflies dance in my stomach. Something about this time seems different. I can't put my finger on what's different, but it is. There's another shoe about to drop any minute now. I know why I'm here. I let *it* get away and now I'm being called out, again. I try to keep it under wraps. I've only let it slip a few times but this last one was a bit of a doozy.

"Well," she says, locking her eyes on mine. "You're nineteen now."

"Yeah…" I say, unsure what the statement is supposed to mean.

I've got until I'm twenty to stay here in the orphanage and it's not like I've got any place else to go. The world has gone to hell-in-a-hand-basket the last ten years. The Horsemen and angels running rampant were only the start. Things are so much worse now that Wormwood fell from the sky and the monsters really came out.

"Aviella, you've been quite the topic of discussion," she says, leaning back in her chair.

"Me?" I ask, unable to keep the surprise out of my voice.

*First rule, don't draw attention,* I hear my father's voice in my head.

Thanks dad, not helpful, and it's not like I haven't tried.

"Yes, you," she says, drumming her long, wrinkled fingers on the desk. "Despite our best efforts to help you, you've not adjusted. You have no friends-"

"Who wants them when-" I interrupt but she cuts me off with a glare.

"-to speak of. You're a barely average student. The number of reports…"

She looks down at the thick file in front of her and my stomach sinks through the floor.

"I can explain," I begin, scrambling to find said explanation. I don't really have one. I don't trust people. Any of them, not the other orphans, not the teachers, no one. It's nothing personal, I guess. Dad never left us in one place long enough for me to form attachments and now it's just easier to be alone. I can't risk someone finding out about *it* and if I let someone get close then they might.

Besides most of them are mean, petty, and perpetually cruel. It's the way of the world now. Those who survived the breaking of the Seals have been driven underground. The surface is too dangerous to live on. Yay, life goes on even though it probably shouldn't. What gives us the right?

See, thoughts like that is why no one likes me. They're all making the best of things like it's not so bad. I don't agree. It is bad. Real bad and putting your head in the sand isn't going to fix it. No one wants to hear the blunt truth though. It'd be nice to have a friend, or two, but should I have to completely change who I am for someone to like me?

Matron Bella clears her throat loudly, jerking me out of my circling thoughts. Yeah, that doesn't help with making friends either. Getting lost in my own head makes me come across like a bitch. Where was I? Oh, damn, right an excuse for the reports. Well, start with the last one.

"I didn't do anything this time," I say, nodding emphatically to give credence to my words.

She arches an eyebrow, purses her lips, but doesn't speak so I continue in a rush.

"Lessa and her cronies pushed me into a corner. I'm the victim here really. She was picking on me and then they all ganged up and then-"

Then what Aviella? Then *it* got out from under my control and the next thing I knew Lessa was flying into the wall? Right, tell her that. See how well that works out.

"I don't know what happened."

I shift in the chair trying to ease the pressure on my butt.

"You don't know..." she says, trailing off, fingers drumming on her desk.

We stare at each other in silence. My cheeks burn and I can't meet her gaze. Of course I know what happened. I don't want to tell her but I know. *It* happened. The buzz in my bones started, I got mad, and then boom. It slipped my grasp.

Squirming under her stare, my mouth dries out and it's hard to swallow. Random excuses pop in and out of my thoughts but I discard them as fast as they come.

Face it girl, you're screwed.

"It's not me..." I start, but I catch the deepening of her frown and my train of thought leaves the station without me.

"It never is," she finishes, shaking her head.

"Aviella, we've done all we can for you," she says. "We've decided it's time for you to go out into the world."

My mouth drops open as I stiffen in the chair. My stomach is a heavy weight holding me down. If it wasn't, I might fall to the floor. Deep inside there is the low buzz, reacting to my fear.

"Uh..., uhm..." my mouth moves but I can't form words.

The room spins, and I grab the sides of the hard, wooden chair with both hands, trying to stop my trembling muscles. Suddenly I'm nine years old again, curled in a ball and holding my white rhino, burying my face in my dad's pillow so I can smell him.

Waiting and alone.

Distantly the Matron is still speaking but it's not words, only sounds that make no sense.

*Aviella, you're special. Heaven watches over you,* daddy whispers.

The buzz cuts through everything else. The room stops spinning and everything is crisp and clear, like I'm seeing it for the first time. I notice the scuff marks and wear on every-thing. Manufacturing of new things became almost non-existent after humanity went underground. The desk, the chair, the books, everything is worn. When I look at Matron Bella I can see that she's worn too, but there's a soft white light that emanates from her. It gives her a gentle glow and when I focus on it that light grows brighter. I see in it something pure, something more than what she presents to the world.

Huh, that's new.

"You've been assigned to a bunker," she's saying, the sound from her lips becoming words and making sense at last. "I have that information here and this is your paperwork."

She holds out an envelope stuffed with papers. It's dirt smudged and obviously been used more than once. My hand trembles as I take it. It's heavier than I expect, like judgment being passed down and I've been found wanting. Yay me.

"Okay," I say, swallowing the lump out of my throat.

She smiles, making the white glow around her pulse bright for a moment.

"It's for the best Aviella," she says. "You don't belong here."

"Uh, okay."

Of course I don't belong here. I don't belong anywhere. I've always been the odd girl out. Weird shit has happened around me all my life. You'd think with the world literally gone to hell I'd fit in better but no such luck. I'm still me, still an outcast, and still all alone.

Sighing, I put an end to my own pity party and stand up. Light-headedness passes over me in a fast wave, but I don't let it lay claim. Matron Bella rises to her feet too.

"I'll just be…" I say, waving the envelope around like it's a magic wand that's going to fix everything.

"You'll be fine."

I hear the sincerity in her voice and I know she means it. Another one of the things that makes me oh so popular. I know when someone is lying. Growing up in an orphanage in the apocalypse, calling people out when they're lying isn't good for making friends. Trust me, it sucks. Of course, in this case her conviction that I'll be fine means jack all.

"There are a few credits and a ration card in there for

you. Don't lose them. The ration card is the only way to get food in the Bunkers. You'll want to gather your belongings from your room?"

It's a question. As orphans, none of us have much that is ours and I'm sure a lot of them leave without bothering to look back, but I do have a few things I want.

"Yeah, please," I say.

She motions towards the door of her office. When I pull it open, two large men stand to either side, dressed in threadbare black suits. They glare, carrying their intimidation on their face. The buzz starts in my bones as I look over my shoulder at Matron Bella. She shrugs sheepishly. Seriously, they're that worried about me?

There's a moment I consider making a scene. The noise grows louder and louder. It'd be easy to let *it* go and leave in a style that no one would soon forget. Tempting, so so tempting, but that's not right and I can't. The troubles I've had here are no one's fault but my own. I'm the weird-o after all. Letting out a huff of breath, I square my shoulders, shove the envelope into my back pocket and walk to my quarters, hulking guards in tow.

The halls of the orphanage are strangely empty. I'm in my shared bunk before it strikes me that they've made sure no one will see me leave. I feel like it should bother me, but it doesn't. Matron Bella is right. I don't have any friends here. Crawling into the lower bunk that has been mine these past ten years, I grab my white rhino out of the corner. I stuff him into my shoulder bag then reach under my pillow and pull out the wrinkled photograph stashed there. Dad's smiling face with his arm around a much younger me. Sunshine, green trees and grass, it all seems unreal even though I was there. It's been too long.

You're special Aviella. Heaven will watch out for you.

Your Mother watches over you always, I hear daddy like he's whispering in my ear.

I hope so. Cause I'm on my own, again. Climbing out of my bunk I step out of the small room between my two guards.

"Okay boys," I say. "I came, I saw, and I burned my regrets. You ready?" I quip.

They don't even crack a smile. Tough crowd. One of them takes the lead this time while the other falls in behind me. Extra careful to make sure I don't make a run for it. A run to where is unclear but better safe than sorry when dealing with the crazy girl.

We don't meet another soul on our way out. The heavy metal door with the large wheel grows larger as we make our way down the hallway. It's covered in peeling paint and rust and looks a lot worse than it did ten years ago. When I came through the last time I think I was still in shock. The one in front grabs the wheel and leans into it, straining. A vein pounds in his forehead as he tries until at last he lets go, huffing and puffing. Silently, the other one steps around me and the two of them grab the wheel together. There's a loud screech as it breaks free then it spins followed by metallic clanging. Bending their knees, they pull, and the door slowly slides open with a puff of stale air.

Dim, flickering light illuminates the other side, revealing a long tunnel. My heart pounds in my chest looking out at my future. The air drifting in smells of sweat, urine, and something even more tangy. Unpleasant to say the least. Great, I didn't know the worst part of being kicked out would be the smell. Ugh.

"Don't suppose either of you are looking for a new adventure?" I ask. The two men stare like I spoke some foreign language. "Seriously? Not even a smile? What's a girl got to do for attention?"

Still silent, they move to stand on either side of the door, pointedly crossing their arms over their chests.

"Yeah, yeah, I get the hint."

Taking one last breath of stale orphanage air, I step across the threshold into the tunnel. The door screeches as they swing it shut, then slams into place. A resounding echo bounces away then comes back. After the echo dies away there's something else, a loud screech that makes my skin crawl and a shuddering cold chill run down my spine.

# CHAPTER TWO

*I*t responds to my fear. Buzzing almost loud enough to drown out the horrid screeching. There's an itch deep inside my brain, something I can't put my finger on, like someone is watching me. I struggle to control it, I can't lose control.

Breathe. Focus, inhale, exhale.

The sound grows louder, echoing off the walls and doubling over. The lights flicker, creating crazy shadows.

Okay Aviella, get a hold of yourself.

When everything is bad go forward. Seems like something my dad would say. After all what choice do I really have? So, I go forward. The tunnel is long and empty and the first step is the hardest, after that it's easier. After about fifty steps, the sound stops with a loud clank. There's a moment of silence and then a low buzz of conversation. That sound pulls me forward. It's probably another hundred feet before a tunnel opens up on my left. The voices are coming from that way.

This tunnel is darker and it takes a few minutes for my eyes to fully adjust. It curves around to the right and to the left like it was dug by a drunken miner. As it curves back upon itself again there's a light and the sound of conversation grows louder.

I emerge out of the tunnel onto an old subway platform. A couple dozen people mill around. Some talk to each other while others stare ahead, ignoring those around them. No one looks my way, and for that I'm relieved, but there's still that itching, hair standing up on the back of my neck sensation that I'm being watched. I'm probably being paranoid. Probably. But as my dad used to joke, just because you're paranoid doesn't mean they're not out to get you.

Trying to keep from attracting any attention, I shift from one side of the platform to the other and move to stand among the crowd waiting to load the train. I haven't been outside the orphanage in ten years, and while we were taught about the new world outside our door, seeing it in person is completely different.

The subway train sitting on the tracks is a testament to both human ingenuity and a statement of values in the apocalypse. It's obviously the source of the god-awful sound I'd heard. I remember the subway from before the move underground but it's nothing like this.

The train cars are no longer enclosed. The walls and roof have been cut off, leaving the seats and poles exposed on all sides. It's a platform on wheels. At the head, where the engine used to be, is a platform with a massive two-sided lever. On each side of the lever are six pathetic looking people, male and female. They're dirty, malnourished, and sad looking. My stomach sinks when I notice their feet are shackled to the platform. They're slaves or prisoners or both.

This is what we've come to. Electricity is too expensive and too hard to produce. Human lives are cheap in comparison. I look around but no one else gives the slaves a second glance. It's like they don't exist and maybe for all these people they don't. I can't look away though. What could they have done that was so bad they deserve a fate like this?

The people on the train car finish unloading and those of us waiting to get on move forward. I follow along, moving with the crowd, trying but failing to keep my attention off the slaves at the front. Then my bag is jerked off my shoulder and gone.

"Hey!" I shout.

Anger flashes white hot and the buzz rises with it as I whirl around. A few people look around when I shout but no one moves to help. The thief is running, shoving people out of his way. It is so loud in my ears I can't hear my heart. The thief is getting away.

"Somebody stop him!" I scream.

A few people look at me and then quickly away. I don't know why but somehow that pisses me off even more. I should let it go. It's only things, sure, but all my credits are in that bag.

And my rhino! Oh hell no.

I stop holding *it* back, letting it bubble to the surface. Focusing on the receding back of the thief I pour it out of me, following the line between me and him. I'm going to stop that bastard.

Power burns through my veins like a cleansing fire. It feels good. That's the problem and why it scares me so much. Anytime I let it go, it feels too good. Too right. I'm already an outcast, how bad would it be if I went around flaunting my powers?

My vision narrows down to the thief. I'm about to let it all go with every intention of smashing that bastard to the ground, but someone steps in my way. I jerk back on the power but it's like fighting a high-pressure firehose. It's almost impossible to pull it back.

The hair on my arms stands on end and my head feels like

it's going to explode as I try to keep from hurting someone other than the one I was aiming for. The man who stepped in my way is chasing down the thief. I can't hurt him. That would be terrible.

I can feel my arms and legs shuddering but all my concentration is on trying to contain my power. Having pulled it back, now it's trying to explode out of me in all directions. I bite my lip so hard I taste coppery blood. This is not the way to start my life outside the orphanage. If this gets away all these people are going to get hurt.

"No, no, no, please help me," I whisper.

It's almost like a prayer, or close enough.

A hand grips my shoulder.

"Shit!" I swear, unable to control my reaction without losing control of the power I'm struggling to contain.

The hand's grip tightens slightly and my power drains away. It leaves me feeling empty and spent. Nothing like this has ever happened before. I should be afraid, but I'm not. I'm looking into the warm, brown eyes of a man. The moment our eyes meet my heart flutters in my chest and something deep stirs. My mouth goes dry as I take in his strong features. A high forehead with his hair cut short on the sides and thick on top. He has a full beard too and an intensity to his gaze that makes me want to fall into him.

"You were about to lose your temper," he says with half grin.

"Who?" I can't finish the line, my mind goes blank.

"You should really avoid doing that around here."

His aura is highly magnetic and compelling. I'm drawn into his words. It feels like the world around me has shifted into a dream. It's an effort of will to focus. He knew I was about to lose my temper and it. How?

"Right," I say. "Uh, you are?"

"Me? I'm Killian. Ronan's on his way back with your purse."

"It's not a purse," I say defensively.

He smiles in a way that pisses me off. It's infuriating and enticing all at the same time.

"Not a purse, okay, he says, looking past me.

I would argue. I want to disagree. Mostly I realize I just want to keep him talking. There's something about him that calls to me. A kindred spirit or something.

"Seriously," I say, putting my hands on my hips. "It's a shoulder bag."

He glances down at me with that same infuriating, ear-to-ear grin. "Okay, well Ronan will be back in a moment with your bag."

I resist the urge to slap that smile off his face, only because I'd have to touch his soft looking beard and once I started I might not be able to stop. And that would lead all kinds of distractions I don't have time for. In order to take my attention off of Killian, I turn and watch Ronan chase down the thief.

The one I assume is Ronan is running behind the fleeing figure. He has a close shaved head and I can see the tail end of a tattoo coming around the back. He moves through the crowd with an ease that's almost supernatural. People seem to just get out of his way without him having to do anything.

The thief glances back over his shoulder and his eyes widen. Ronan leaps forward and if I didn't know better I would swear he was half angel. He glides through the air, impossibly far, to land right behind the thief and grab him by the neck. Ronan lifts the other man off the ground and the thief pulls back a fist, obviously intending to swing, but when he meets Ronan's gaze his hand drops to his side.

"Here," the thief says holding up my bag. "Take it. Please just don't hurt me."

Ronan says something that I can't hear as he puts the man back on his feet. They don't exchange another word. The thief turns and walks away and Ronan heads back towards Killian and me.

As he gets closer I get a strange sense of déjà vu. His eyes. There's something about his eyes. They're rich emerald, like reflective pools and when Ronan smiles the familiarity grows stronger.

"I know you," I insist in shock and confusion.

Ronan looks past me at Killian before meeting my gaze again. He holds my bag out in front of him, bowing his head as he offers it to me. I take it with numb fingers. He doesn't say anything in response though. I stare at him, trying to place how or where I know him.

"How about we buy you lunch?" Killian asks, interrupting my thoughts.

As if on cue my stomach grumbles. I open my mouth to say no but something else completely comes out

"Okay," I agree.

The two handsome men smile and move to stand on either side of me. They lead the way through the crowd and down the platform. Along the far wall, previously hidden by the crowd, are a series of small booths. One of them is a food stand. As we take our place in line, I look around. The other stalls offer small amenities. One has toiletries and other vital necessities. Another sells small knickknacks that supposedly ward off various bad things like demons.

"How can anybody believe that?" I voice the thought in my head before I can stop my mouth.

Ronan glances in the direction I'm looking and shrugs. "They need something."

"But that's nothing. It's a lie. They're being taken advantage of and it isn't right."

"What would you give them to believe in?" Ronan asks.

It surges up inside, like it's going to bubble out of my skin. It's hard to breathe. All I can think about is those poor souls being suckered. The injustice of it leaves me angry but somehow cold. I don't know how to fix it but I want to.

"Anything, anything but a lie," I say.

"Is it a lie if they believe it?" Ronan asks.

I can feel Killian's eyes on us as we debate but he doesn't say anything. We shuffle forward in line. My power continues to swell and it's becoming harder and harder to contain it.

"Of course it's a lie," I retort. "It doesn't matter if they believe it. That doesn't make it right. If anything, it makes it more wrong. That guy over there is taking advantage of people."

Ronan's green eyes catch mine. He purses his lips before nodding. "It's not that you're wrong," he says. "It's just that you don't understand."

I'm shaking. Every hair on my arms stands on end, crackling with electrical power. This is bad. I have to control this. I can't let it go. The person standing behind the booth selling the knickknacks looks over like he knows something is up.

"We'd better calm this down," Killian says.

"It's. Not. Right," I say, punctuating every word.

"I know," Killian says. "But this isn't the way."

His hand comes down on my shoulder and the power drains away leaving an instant calm. I whirl around towards him, jerking my shoulder out from under his hand.

"What did you do?" I demand.

In the stress of losing my bag, I didn't realize that the draining calm had been Killian's doing. Now I know. Somehow he's like me. Special, different, an outcast.

He smiles, shaking his head and raises both hands in front of himself. "It's nothing," he says. "Seriously everything is fine."

"What'll it be," the attendant behind the counter asks.

His timing is impeccable, cutting through what I want to say. Killian turns to him and orders a bowl of nutri-aid stew. Ronan says he'll have the same and with nothing else to go on I add one for me too.

The attendant quickly serves up three bowls and grabbing one each, we turn away. Ronan leads us to a nearby table and we all sit. He and Killian put all of their attention on the food, eating like they haven't had a meal in forever.

I eat more slowly, watching them warily. I guess some part of me knew that they were like me. Special, with some kind of powers. On the one hand it's like I found friends. Maybe that's why I'm drawn to them. But on the other hand, it makes me even more cautious. If they have powers, maybe running into each other wasn't an accident. Could they be stalking me? Do they have nefarious plans for me?

I hope not. I'd hate to have to hurt them.

Even if I would hate it I would do it.

I can't help staring at Ronan. I'm trying to place him. There something about him that's so familiar. Just when I think I'm about to figure it out, two more men walk up and without asking take seats at our table. I'm more than a bit taken aback.

The first of them has mocha skin, a goatee, and dreadlocks. He has an easy smile and bright, shining eyes. Dressed in a loose, white shirt with bead necklaces around his neck. He takes a seat next to Killian and without asking takes his bowl and starts eating.

The second man has aqua blue eyes and a vague, kind of dreamy look on his face. He has shoulder length blonde hair in a thick bristly beard of the same color. He's wearing a tight black shirt that shows off how fit he is underneath it. He stares at me openly as he takes a seat next to Ronan.

"Find another stray?" the one with dreadlocks asks. He shoots a grin in my direction.

"She's more than a stray," Ronan says.

"I'll say," dreadlocks says. "She's cute."

My power swells in indignation at his words.

His eyes widen and so does his grin. "Oh! Nice."

Is he reacting to my power? It sure seems like it. What are these four?

"Gavin, meet Aviella. Aviella this is Gavin. This other one is Luca."

"Hi," I say, feeling lost and out of place.

Obviously they all know each other. I can't shake the feeling that I should know Ronan but if I know him does that mean they were looking for me? That thought makes me cold. My life is built on flying under the radar, not bringing attention to myself. Attention is bad.

Plus, they know things they shouldn't, that they can't possibly know.

"Your place or Mayan?" Gavin says, smiling even bigger.

Wow. That was a super lame apocalypse pick up line. Luca snorts. Killian groans and Ronan shakes his head.

"You're terrible," Ronan says.

"Hey, what's the point if you can't poke fun at it?" Gavin asks.

"Who are you people?"

The four men exchange a look. It's obvious how well they know each other. Ronan looks over, the haunting green of his eyes boring into me. Suddenly I remember. The day the seals were breaking! He was the boy!

"You threw the rock!" I exclaim.

"What's this?" Gavin asks.

"Nothing," Ronan shrugs.

"It wasn't nothing," I argue. Excitement bubbles up inside me now that I can finally place his face. "You distracted that angel. Without you I wouldn't have gotten by."

Ronan grins before turning his attention to his soup.

"That's our Ronan," Lucas says, speaking for the first time. "Always going for the girl."

"I was nine years old!" I exclaim.

Luca snorts again and returns his attention to the food. Gavin looks back and forth between Ronan and me. "Did you know this Killian?" Gavin asks.

"Nope," Killian answers.

"Keeping secrets are we Ronan?" Gavin asks.

"We have a job to do here," Ronan says, pointedly ignoring the question.

"Well," I say, staring at Ronan pointedly. "Thank you."

"No problem," he says, meeting my gaze.

Strangely I feel comfortable. It's almost like I fit in. It's not a feeling I've ever had before. I'm studying the four men while doing my best to look like I'm doing anything but that. The tattoo around Ronan's head is an intricate design. It's almost like it's different every time I look at it. If I move my eyes along it then go back to where I was just looking it seems like it's changed. I can't put my finger on it.

My heart skips in my chest. There's something about him. Something about all of them. They have an energy that resonates with the thing inside of me but where it is more chaotic and uncontrolled, what I feel in them is organized and clean. It's nice.

"Well Ronan is right," Gavin says, slapping his hands on the table. "Wrap it up boys we have work to do."

The other three stand. As they do, Killian's loose fitting shirt shifts and I catch a corner of a tattoo that looks almost exactly like Ronan's on the right side of his chest. Gavin rises and stretches, causing his shirt to pull up and reveal not only the most perfect abs I've ever imagined but he has the same tattoo on his left side. How strange. I wonder if Luca has one too?

The four of them are looking at me and I realize I'm still sitting here staring and thinking about their tattoos. Socially awkward wins the day, again, go me. I rise from the table, the situation suddenly awkward which is much more in line with what I'm used to. This at least feels normal.

"Thanks for the food."

"Not a problem," Killian says.

It's probably just in my head but it seems like all four of them keep looking at me in a strange, knowing way.

"We have to go," Lucas says.

At about that time, a conductor calls out for the train to be boarded. The four of them turn and saunter away.

"Watch that temper," Killian says over his shoulder, shooting me a grin.

"I'll try," I reply.

"We'll see you again," Gavin assures me then laughs loudly.

The sound of it echoes off the concrete walls. The crowd seems to part around them and soon they disappear, leaving me alone. The emptiness that I'm so familiar with comes back. Well, here I am.

Boarding the train with a sense of trepidation, I find a seat. I look down the line at the slaves who power the journey and my stomach twists into knots. Life wasn't great in the orphanage, but it wasn't like I was living with the Dursley's. In there they protected us while trying to prepare us for the world out here.

Gavin's words play over and over in my mind. What did he mean they'll see me again? Who or what are they? Why do they have the same tattoos? And their energy! It's so clean, controlled. Does that mean they have powers too? Powers they can control? It sure seemed like it. Killian touched me and it went quiet. That's never happened before.

Someone squeezes into the small space beside me, forcing me to try and take up even less space than I already was. The rail car jerks, squeals loudly, then starts into motion. I try not to look but I can't stop myself. My eyes drift, like on their own volition, to the slaves. The haggard people lean into the handle, forcing it up and down. Two guards stand watch, tapping sticks on their legs out of boredom or to imply a threat. It makes me sick to my stomach.

I don't know what I'm going to do when I get to my assigned bunker. I'm all alone with no one I can trust and I miss my dad.

CHAPTER THREE

*H*and-painted signs on the broken concrete walls guide me towards Bunker E247. It doesn't take long, I wander through old subway tunnels before I'm standing at a heavy steel door. Like everything in the apocalypse, the door has seen better days. The faded white paint labeling it is barely readable. There are deep gouges in the steel, where it looks like something monstrous tried to get in. I suppose I should consider it reassuring that whatever was trying to didn't.

In the middle of the door hangs a large iron ring. Since there's no sign of a handle I grab the ring and lift. It's heavy enough that I just let it go and it slams down with a resounding crash.

I wait a few minutes and when nothing happens I lift and let go again. This time there's a response. A scratching sound and then a clang before the door swings open, surprisingly silent.

"Travel papers," a large burly man barks.

I hand him the papers that were given to me by the orphanage. He brings them in close to his face and looks them over carefully before grunting and stepping aside. I cross the threshold and hold my hand up for my papers. He gives them back and returns his attention to closing the door.

When it shuts there's a soft echo that almost seems like the closing of a chapter of my life.

The burly man sits on a stool next to the door, leans back against the wall, and closes his eyes. I look around, uncertain what I'm supposed to do now.

"Uh, excuse me?" I ask, trying to get his attention.

His feet slam to the ground as his eyes open and he glares. "What?"

"Where do I go?"

"Go to intake," he says, crossing his arms across his chest.

I look around, hoping to spot a sign or some other indication of where intake might be. Nothing stands out. Of course it doesn't. Why should anything be any better than before.

The large man must see my confusion. "Damn newbies," he mutters as he rises to his feet. He points down the hall we're standing in. "Hundred feet that way then look left."

Then he just stares.

"Got it."

"Good," he says, resuming his seat.

I follow his directions and about one hundred feet down there's an opening into a small office. There doesn't seem to be anybody around at the desk, so I stand and look around, hoping somebody will notice me. I don't know how long I'm there before an elderly woman walks out is startled at the sight of me.

"Oh, hello," she says.

"Hi. I need to get assigned a bunk?"

"Hmmm," she mutters, frowning.

She pulls out a stack of papers and together we go over all of them. Even in the apocalypse there's no end to the red tape. Maybe it's just something that gives people a sense of purpose. We spend hours filling out document after document. When at last we're done, the old woman grabs the stack and shoves them under the counter.

"You have your ration card?" she asks.

"Yes ma'am."

"Good," she says. She hands me a stiff piece of paper which has a crudely drawn map on it. Running her finger along it, she traces the route, explaining how to reach my bunk.

"Got it?" she asks.

"Yes."

"Okay, good luck." She turns without another word and shuffles back out of sight.

I guess I'll follow the crude map towards my new home.

Before the fall this was a subway. After the apocalypse, the subway became the starting point for the bunkers. The nice, smooth concrete of the former subway comes to an end about another hundred feet down the tunnel at what was a wall. Now it has a crude doorway broken out of it with strips of dried leather hang over the opening. Stepping through, I get my first full view of my new home.

There's an open-air market in the crudely cut out cavern. Makeshift stalls are scattered around haphazardly. There's a quiet murmur of conversation as people barter. Hundreds of people are moving about and for a moment I want to turn around and run away. So many strangers. So many people who might find out I'm different. Bracing myself and taking a deep breath, I walk forward because I have nothing to walk back to.

My first task is to find my bunk. I wander between the stalls, different merchants eyeing me as I go by but apparently realizing I have nothing to trade and quickly losing interest. I don't know how to find my way around here.

There are no obvious signs or signals telling me which way to go.

I stop at a stall that has little pieces of stone carved into the shape of angels. I pick one up and turn it over in my hand. It's strangely warm to the touch.

"Half a day," the merchant says.

"Excuse me?"

"Half a day," he repeats, like that clarifies anything.

Maybe the look of confusion on my face finally gets through to him. He shakes his head, points at the object in my hand, then points at me.

"Half a day's credit," he says. "That's how much it cost."

"What's half a day's credit?"

"Your food credit!" he replies, exasperation on his face and in his voice.

"Oh!" I say, setting the object back on the table. "Thanks, but no thanks."

I turn and walk away, wandering among the stalls for a while longer before I notice arrows and numbers scratched into the floor. Something about that clicks and I realize it lines up with the crude map I was given. That's how I'm supposed to guide my way around down here.

Following the arrows and consulting my map, I work my way through the crowds of people and down several rough-hewn hallways with a lot of twists and turns. There are large rooms cut out of the solid rock. Each one is filled to the brim with bunk beds and people.

The sad, haunted looks on their faces hurts. I try not to let it become depressing.

When I find the bunk room I'm assigned to, it's mostly empty. I carefully pick my way through until I find the bottom bunk I'm assigned to. A girl lying on the top bed sits up when I approach.

"Hi," I greet her.

She smiles and it lights up her entire face. She's got beautiful warm brown eyes and long, thick, luxurious curly brown hair that almost seems unruly as it cascades down across her shoulders. She's wearing a halter top and her turquoise bracelet covered wrists jangle as she waves. She nods her head enthusiastically but doesn't say anything.

"It looks like we're going to be bunkmate's," I say, feeling awkward.

She nods and motions at the bunk below her. I set my bag down and stand, shifting foot to foot, wondering what I've screwed up since she's not talking.

"So...," I say trailing off.

She jumps down from the bunk to stand in front of me, placing both her hands on my shoulders. Instinctively, I lean back and away but my reaction doesn't bother my new bunkmate at all. She grips my shoulders, nods, and then lets them go. Placing a hand on her mouth she taps her face three times and then shakes her head side to side.

"You can't talk?" I ask and she nods. "Oh, I'm sorry. I didn't know."

I try to backpedal, realizing I've been a jerk. Well done Aviella. Like she knows what I'm thinking. she puts a hand on my cheek, smiles, and shakes her head again. Then she reaches into her pocket and pulls out a piece of paper. Her hands seem to fly and in moments the piece of paper is a beautiful dove that she holds out to me.

"Peace offering, huh?" I ask, unable to suppress a grin of my own.

She nods and in that moment I know I've found a friend. That's a first for me.

My new bunkmate pulls out another piece of paper and a short stub of a pencil. She scribbles on the paper, holding it on the palm of her hand. Finishing she holds it up.

Rowan.

Looking at it then her, it purrs, similar to my power's reaction to the men at the subway station.

"Rowan? That's you?" I ask and she nods. "Hi. I'm Aviella."

She holds out her hand and I take it. An electric buzz passes between us, it's not unpleasant, just strange. Rowan looks at our hands, smiles bigger, then pulls me into a tight embrace. It takes a moment, but I relax and return the hug.

AFTER THREE WEEKS OF LIVING IN THE BUNKER MY LIFE IS becoming routine. While at first it was completely foreign, now I find it's not so different from life in the orphanage. The biggest change is that I actually have a friend. Something I never managed before.

Our room in the bunker definitely has its fair share of colorful people. And by colorful, I mean crazy. There's one guy that we refer to as the governor. He's always dressed in a ratty suit but carries himself around with an air of authority and power that he has no claim to. He tends to give long and involve diatribes about what we should all be doing and how we should all be acting. I'm sure before the apocalypse he was a politician. Now he's just daft.

"And that is why we all have to work together. If all of you would just stand with me, we could take over this entire bunker. There's no reason that we shouldn't have equal treatment," the governor says, standing on a wooden box he has set up in the middle of our room.

He gestures broadly, using his hands to emphasize his words. Dozens of us are watching his speech but not for him or his words. Rowan stands five feet behind him, mimicking his gestures in an exaggerated manner that's absolutely hilarious. All of us watching are doing our best not to laugh so we don't ruin the show. One thing I've learned so far about life in the bunker is: you take entertainment anywhere you can find it.

The funniest part is the governor actually thinks we're listening to him and responding to his speech. It only encourages him to go further. It makes me realize how lucky I am to have found Rowan.

The single light in our bunk flickers, casting shadows around the room. A moment later the rattle of locust wings fills the air. Even this far underground they're loud.

Rowan stops, dropping her arms to her side. Everyone else stops too, looking up at the ceiling. There's no way the locusts can get in here. Were safe. No one says a word, too terrified to make a sound. Locusts hunt by sound.

Quiet as a mouse, Rowan walks over and sits on the bunk next to me. We grab each other's hands and squeeze tight. The only way they could get in is if somebody left the door open and nobody is that crazy. They'd have to be absolutely insane. Suicidal.

There's a sinking feeling in my stomach as the light switches off. Instinctively, I reach out for my dad. It doesn't matter how long he's been gone, in moments like this I still want him. There's an empty ache inside of me where he should be.

I blink away tears, thankful it's dark so no one can see. Like she knows, Rowan puts an arm around my shoulders and pulls me close and we hold each other for a long moment as the sound of wings continues.

No one dares breath a sound. Fear is heavy in the room, mingling with the odors of sweat and unwashed bodies. Water is almost as scarce as food in the bunker. The swarm above must be huge. Sometimes they take a day or more to pass over, during which we have to remain as silent as possible. Sure there's a big door blocking us from the locusts but why tempt fate?

After a while it becomes obvious that there's not going to be an end to the swarm anytime soon. Rowan squeezes me tight then climbs up into her own bunk. Lying down in mine, I can't keep my thoughts away from my dad.

I resolved myself to the fact that he's gone a long time ago, although there's still some silly part of me that holds out hope. Hope that he might be out there somewhere still alive, still looking for me. It's silly and childish but whatever.

The best thing I can do now is go to sleep. Rolling over onto my side, I wrap my arms tightly around myself and remember a trick dad showed me to help me sleep. Growing up, when the bombs were still falling, he taught me to repeat a mantra over and over in my head. It helped me build a safe place where I could block out the horrors of the world around us.

He always said it was a trick my mother taught him. I don't know if that's true or not, but I do remember it works. When the apocalypse started, the Army tried to go to war against the Angels and Demons. They had no idea how badly out manned they were. Their bombs and guns were next to useless. No one was prepared for what came, how could they be?

So many nights I would drift off to sleep to the sounds of people screaming outside. Dad was always so calm. He was prepared and nothing seemed to faze him. He knew how to survive. It's that fact alone that leaves me hope, even if it's just a glimmer.

MY EYES SNAP OPEN, HALF AWAKE, STILL HALF ASLEEP. Remnants of a dream intrude upon the world around me. I can't sort out what's real and what's nightmare.

I see demons leading an undead army that's branded with

a strange sigil. They're marching ahead, breaking down the doors to bunkers. People are screaming, dying. My heart pounds and I want to cry out, but my throat is closed tight. A hand clenches my shoulder, turning me around.

Silvery violet eyes stare into mine. Cold fear sends chills through me but then I realize it's not a demon. Shit, I'm sleepwalking and still can't discern what's real. This must be part of the dream. I stumble forward, guided by the hand on my shoulder until I'm lying in my bunk and darkness returns.

~

THE MONOTONY OF BUNKER LIFE PLODS ON UNTIL ONE morning Rowan is next to my bunk, bouncing from foot to foot and twirling, holding something in her hand. She waves it like it's a magic wand.

Sitting up on the edge of the bed, I stretch and yawn before turning my attention towards figuring out what's in her hand, blinking the sleep from my eyes until I can focus. She's holding up a rations ticket.

"It's delivery day?"

Rowan nods, enthusiastic as ever. Ration day means that for at least a week we'll eat better than for the rest of the month.

Protective Services, the remnants of the former govern-ment, distributes food to all the bunkers. Theoretically they keep everyone on equal footing. In reality, life in the bunkers is anything but equal. There are bunkers that are considered the lands of plenty. Home to those who were wealthy and powerful before the apocalypse so now they get advantages no one else does.

Wiping the sleep from my eyes, I climb out of bed. I've

never been a morning person, but Rowan's enthusiastic nature is infectious.

"Well okay, let's do this," I say, putting an arm around her shoulders.

Together we walk out of our bunk and head towards the marketplace. The hallways are filled with people and the buzz of excitement. Rations day is a bright spot in an otherwise monotonous and dull life. Surprisingly, despite the large crowds, most people are amicable. There isn't a lot of pushing or shoving as we work our way into the market.

It's hard to tell if that's because people are actually nice or because on ration day there are armed guards overseeing the distribution. The cynical part of me believes it's the latter. I'm sure if Rowan could speak she would say it was the former. She's ever the optimist. I guess in that way we are like Yin and Yang, opposites attract.

One wall of the marketplace has been taken over for distribution and is lined with wooden tables. On top of each are buckets filled with rations. A sign hangs on the front of each bucket telling you how many credits it will take you to purchase it.

There's a person stationed at each table to take your credits and behind every one is an armed guard. I make my selections carefully as I go down the line. Focusing on basics and things that I can stretch out for the month. One bucket has real meat and I look at it longingly. In the orphanage we got real meat twice a month. I haven't had any since I left because I haven't been assigned any work, so I'm on a bare minimum of credits. Maybe next month I'll get a job and afford it.

Reaching the end of the line, my bag is filled with enough food to get me by. It's all about survival in the apocalypse. Anything else is bonus.

"The crowd's really heavy back the way we came," I say to Rowan. "How about we take the long way home?"

She smiles and nods, her curly hair bouncing. Hefting my bag over my shoulder I lead the way out of the crowds into the main marketplace and over to a nearby tunnel. It will loop around and come up behind our bunk.

When we turn a corner, there's a shifty looking man standing in the middle of the tunnel with his arms crossed over his chest. He has dark eyes and as soon as I see him the buzz begins inside my bones. Even Rowan loses her perpetual smile.

"This tunnel has a toll," he says, voice low and threatening.

"That wasn't mentioned during intake."

He grits his teeth, shaking his head. My hands ball into fists as the buzz grows louder. The jerk leans forward in an obviously threatening motion.

"We'll have to make sure that gets added to the orientation," he says, raising his hands before him. "Now open up those bags and let me see what you got."

My outrage at the situation is making it difficult to hold on to the power surging through me. It would be so easy to let it go. I can see him in my mind's eye being tossed around like a paper doll on a thunderstorm. Gritting my teeth, I try to keep it under control. If I let it go, I'll be exposed. Everyone will know that I'm different. I'll be in way more danger than I am right now.

"I'm not going to do that," I say, my voice tight.

Sweat forms on my brow and my muscles are shaking. The buzz is so loud now I can barely hear my own voice.

"I told you to bring me with you. The bags are too heavy," a new voice says.

It jerks my attention away from my struggle to control the power. An incredibly handsome man has walked up next to us. He glances over at me and familiar silver-violet eyes

48

stare into mine. They can't be real, those are the same eyes I dreamed of last night.

It's obvious he's not like the others. I don't know how I know, it's just a feeling. In some way it's like he and I are cut from the same cloth. There's an air of danger about him. I look from him to the would-be thief. There's something in his eyes encouraging me to play along. Glancing over at Rowan, she smiles and shakes her head, then shrugs.

Why not? I might as well play along. "Well you were taking too long," I say to the newcomer.

"Isn't that just like a woman?" he asks with a sly grin. "No patience." He looks over at the rogue.

The rogue looks between the two of us, crestfallen. He steps back once then twice without turning around.

"What about your toll?" I'm unable to resist asking.

He doesn't speak, shaking his head side to side as he continues to walk backwards until the tunnel branches off to either side and he dodges to the left, running out of sight.

With the immediate threat gone, I turn my full attention on the newcomer. As soon as I do, I feel a sharp current of energy focus on me. It reminds me of when my father used to leave the view screens on at night. There's a hum that passes over my skin and the hair on my arms stands on end. It only takes a second to realize he's scanning me.

I'm not sure how I know that's what he's doing. And then it hits me, I do the exact same thing every time I meet a new person. It's instinctual for me and it probably is for him as well. Yet more proof that we are cut from the same cloth.

He takes the bag off my shoulder without a word then steps over the Rowan and takes hers too. Neither of us resist, one because he's been helpful, and two the bags actually are heavy.

"Hi, I'm Efram. Want to lead the way?"

I exchange a look with Rowan and she shrugs noncommittally. Thanks Rowan, real helpful.

"Uh, sure. I'm Aviella, this is Rowan."

He accompanies us all the way to our bunk and puts our bags down on the bunk. When I turn to face him, I get a good look and my heart skips a beat. He's incredibly handsome and there's something, some kind of a connection between the two of us. Something I can't put my finger on.

"Thank you," I say. Rowan nods and motions with her hands to him. "Rowan wants to thank you also."

"It's not a problem," he says.

Rowan looks between the two of us and her smile grows wider. Silently she walks away, leaving me alone with him. I sigh, thanks Rowan.

"Avoid it if you can but learn to fight. Innocence is a delicacy here," Efram says.

Huh? Totally not what I expected him to say.

"Yeah, okay."

He stares at me for a long moment and not having anywhere else to look the moment becomes awkward. I don't know what to say or do. Outside of Rowan this is probably one of the longest interactions I've had with another human being that didn't end with me hurting them somehow.

"I'll see you around," he says, turning and walking away.

I watch him go, wanting to say something but having no idea what. It leaves me feeling lost. Wanting to focus on something besides my confused feelings, I put away both mine and Rowan's food supplies. Someone in our room has an old, staticky radio playing some kind of talk radio. It crackles, the voice fading in and out so that I can't make out actual words. It's mostly background noise.

I lie down on my bunk and consider what Efram said. I do need to learn how to fight. If I could master the power inside of me and truly control it, no one would ever be able to hurt Rowan or me. I'd always be able to keep us safe. Maybe Efram could teach me if I told him what I can do. That wouldn't be so bad would it? Opening up to another and being truly honest with someone.

No, it's better I keep to myself. If my father taught me nothing else, he taught me that. I guess I could try and teach myself how to fight, somehow.

Trying to take my thoughts off the stranger, I pull out a book that I borrowed from the bunker library and try to lose myself in it. I've only read a couple of pages when the lights flicker. I freeze as the sounds of locust wings echo through the tunnels. A heartbeat later the radio shuts off and the lights go out. Curling into a ball I wait.

# CHAPTER FOUR
## EFRAM

*I*'m thankful that there are no bodies to interrogate tonight. I can't get that girl out of my head. There's something about her that worms its way into my thoughts. She's going to get eaten alive without someone looking out for her. And I can sense her power. It calls to me.

In all my life I've never felt anyone with more raw power. When I was near her I could feel it crawling across my skin, exotic, enticing, and I can't get it out of my head. She restrains herself, doesn't embrace the power. It's almost like she's afraid of it.

I'm worried it's not enough to keep her safe from the dangers of bunker society. Her innocence is palpable and cautious, like she's known deep suffering, and somehow managed to preserve her heart.

I want to take her under my wing, but I'm not sure I can. It's too dangerous to open myself up that way. Memories of my sister, Jenna, rise unbidden and I grit my teeth as I enter the administrator's office. That's is exactly what I don't want to remember.

I scan over the board for new jobs. Anything to keep my

mind off Aviella. My eyes land on one, a transport run looking for a loader. It's a bad news assignment, looting a bunker that fell to a locust swarm. I rip it off the board and shove it in my pocket, but I feel like I can't leave the bunker. I can't let Aviella be on her own.

This is insane, I have to work. How can this girl have insinuated herself so deeply into my thoughts? I don't know her. Yet somehow it feels right, like I'm meant to be around just for her.

The floor creaks behind me and I turn, eye to eye with Rafe.

His golden eyes reflect the light when he holds up a tattooed hand and smiles. "Got another body for you," he says. "It pays double for specifics."

So much for no bodies tonight.

## CHAPTER FIVE

*T*he bunker radio is playing an upbeat jazz, like the more frequent locust visits are nothing to worry about. It's a grating contrast to memories of my nightmares that beat incessantly against my thoughts. They come every single night and always involve the undead. It's distressing and it means I'm running short on sleep.

Once upon a time sleep was a refuge, an escape. It's really unfair that the nightmare has now invaded my sanctuary. Even my dad's trick for building a wall in my mind doesn't help. It feels like something is coming. That's silly though, how could I possibly know that?

I focus all my attention on the old, carved wood puzzle I'm building on my bed. Rowan found it in the lost and found, a special room of the bunker where they put unclaimed items from those who have died. My thoughts keep trying to drift to things I don't want to think about and I keep having to jerk them back, the puzzle is helping me block everything out.

Old things like the puzzle have an appeal to me. Picking

up a piece and trying to find where it fits, it's warm in my hands like there's a bit of energy trapped inside. Almost like it's a part of an era that's been preserved and reminds me of better times.

Rowan hangs her head over the edge of her bunk, looking in on me and her bright smile lifts my spirits. I know she's seen hardships but nothing gets her down. No matter how bad things are, she's a bright light shining in the apocalypse. I respect her for that. She's my best friend, my only friend, the only one I've ever had.

Angry voices come through the door and into our room. Concern flashes in Rowan's eyes. The voices outside get louder and my pulse quickens, something bad is happening. We live in a remote corner of the bunker. Bad things happen back here all the time. Common sense tells me not to get involved, it's not my problem, but Rowan's mouth tightens and the concern in her eyes grows. She's right. Despite my apprehension, somebody has to do something. No one else in our room makes a move though, so I guess it all comes down to me.

Climbing out of my bed, I walk over to the door and throw it open. A striking man is holding another man aloft by his neck. A spike of fear jolts through me only to be followed up by... desire? At a time like this? Seriously Aviella get a hold of yourself.

Ignoring my body's idiocy, I step outside the door and the aggressor glances at me. His eyes can't seriously be glowing crimson, can they? He blinks and his eyes are a normal, golden brown. I recognize the man he's holding aloft, a known thief, but so is pretty much everyone in the bunker.

"Hey!" I call. It doesn't matter that the man's a thief, nobody deserves to die over it.

Golden eyes stares at me for a long, uncomfortable

moment. Long enough for me to notice his thick, pretty lashes that go really well with his long, brown hair. He wears it shaved and braided on one side revealing tattoos that crawl up his neck.

"See that?" he says, still watching me but talking to the thief. "You got an angel looking out for you, today, Brody. Empty your pockets and you walk away."

I watch as Brody retrieves wads of food tickets he's stolen and I shake my head. Maybe I shouldn't have intervened. How many people has the creep stolen food from? No rations means death in the bunker. Pretty boy snatches them from the thief's hand and puts Brody back on the floor before turning towards me with a grin. I can feel his mental scan.

"Just keepin' the neighborhood clean ma'am," he says, bowing without taking his eyes off of mine.

His cocky grin makes stupid, girlish butterflies flutter in my lower belly. I seriously almost groan out load. My face flushes hot with embarrassment which only makes him smile wider. Straightening, he mocks a hat tip towards me and strolls away.

I must have been channeling Rowen with my mute act there. When I turn to go back into the room, she's standing with a silly smile on her face.

"What?"

She looks down the hallway in the direction the guy left and then back at me. I roll my eyes.

"You can't be serious."

Rowan wiggles her eyebrows up and down.

"He was going to hurt that other guy," I protest, exasperated.

Rowan holds her hands up in front of her and shakes her head like she's saying 'take what you can get'. I shake my head in response and push past her towards our bunks, grabbing a voucher from my stuff.

"I'm going to take a shower," I tell Rowan.

She nods, smiles and then pitches her nose.

"You know you don't smell any better right?"

Rowan laughs. When she laughs she doesn't make any sound, but it shakes her whole body, her eyes light up, and her face glows with joy. There's something special about it.

I make my way down the tunnel to the community showers. I hand over my voucher and they let me in. Just inside is a double row of sinks set facing each other so that when you're using one you're staring straight at the person across from you. Water is carefully rationed, coming out in small bursts so I quickly brush my teeth and head for the showers.

Water is perhaps the biggest luxury of all. Between all the nuclear bombs and the Wormwood event, not only is the surface an inhabitable wasteland, the water supplies have all been poisoned.

Stepping into the small stall, I turn on the water and immediately get hit with a blast of cold. Great, I think, trying to catch my breath. The heaters are out again.

If nothing else it inspires me to shower faster and I wrap up as quickly as possible, dry off with my thin, threadbare towel, and head back to my bunk.

Rowan is standing at the end of our bunks stirring a little pot of beans on the portable camp cooker we share. She grins when I enter and motions me over. She's already gotten out the flatbread she and I created from our combined Nutrimeal rations. She picks one up, cupping it in her hands, and fills it with savory beans. Once she's finished, she hands it to me and I take it gratefully, quickly wolfing down the food. It's not particularly tasty but it is filling.

Rowan is already done and playing solitaire on her bed, completely consumed by it. She never seems to have problems concentrating like I do. When she fixates on something, there's no breaking her away from it.

Having nothing else to do I curl up on my bed. I can't keep my thoughts away from the men I've met recently. All of whom I felt a connection with. Is that normal? Do other girls feel this way? Sighing heavily, I pull the book I've been reading out from under my pillow. It's a page worn romance. Probably not the best thing to get my mind off of men, but hey it's all I've got.

It almost feels like we were all destined to meet each other but how can that be a thing? Destiny, it's the kind of fairytale that exists in these books, not here in the real world of the apocalypse.

The characters in the book are dueling over the female's heart. In my mind's eye, they take on the appearance of Efram and the golden-eyed man. As soon as it happens, my cheeks burn hot. It's silly. I don't know what I'm thinking.

A yawn catches me by surprise, so I close the book and tuck it under my pillow. Maybe tonight I'll have happy dreams. Or at least no nightmares, though I won't hold my breath on that. Listening to the crackling buzz of the bunker radio, I drift off to sleep.

I snap awake. Something is wrong. I don't know what, but I sense it. Jumping out of bed, I turn a circle before it clicks. Locust wings. I start to relax but something is off about the sound. What is it?

Rowan sits up in her bed looking around, eyes wide. I shake my head answer to her unasked question. The sound is definitely off.

"They're inside!" I gasp.

The locusts are inside. Before I know what I'm doing, I'm

running out the door. My mind screams for me to stop, but the power inside has taken control. My blood runs hot and a lightning flow of adrenaline dumps into my system. Fearful eyes peer out of their doors, glancing around as I run towards the entrance. When I reach the marketplace and approached the main door, I stop short, paralyzed by fear.

The door is open. Filling it completely is a locust swarm. It's taken on the shape of a massive humanoid. Millions of the evil, mutated creatures are swarming together. A woman stands in front of it, weaving back and forth. She must be the one that opened the door but why? No one in their right mind would open the door.

The buzz in my bones grows louder and my heart pounds in my chest. Knowing it's foolish and I'm probably going to get myself killed, I run straight at the monster. I grab the woman standing in front of it and pull her behind me. The giant bug monster leers, wings clacking like metal bowls.

My powers are overriding my will, it is a surging energy and I know that everyone watching is going to find out my secret. I'm sorry dad.

It doesn't matter, I have to save everyone.

My head is pounding and I'm hot, so damn hot. Focusing on the thing in front of me, I try to let the power go. It's the way it's always worked before but instead of a powerful force blasting out of me, words come out of my mouth. It's a tongue. I don't even know what I'm saying. Strange, ancient and almost alien but the locust monster backs up, starting to lose its shape.

I point at it as more words spew from my lips. The swarming locust loses its shape and collapses into individual insects. Each of them a horror with little human faces, rows of razor sharp teeth, hard shells that are almost impossible to break, and claws that are just as sharp as their teeth.

Having lost its shape, the swarm also loses its direction.

It's now a swirling cloud hanging just outside the door. Something pushes through it. Another massive, horrid thing that shouldn't exist. It's an undead monstrosity. There are empty, gaping holes where its eyes should be. It stumbles through the cloud of locusts, heading straight for me. The buzzing in my head grows louder and I focus, about to unleash it but something stops me. It won't go. I don't know why.

The monstrosity comes closer, rotten flesh falling off its arm as it grasps.

It's just about to touch me.

I'm frozen in place, can't move, can't do anything.

My stomach flips in horror.

Suddenly, someone pushes past me.

"Not this one," the newcomer says.

It's the golden-eyed, tattooed man! What the hell is he doing here?

The dead thing shuffles like it's going to push past but then stops and looks. If I didn't know better I'd say the thing was confused and afraid. Can dead things be afraid?

I guess if the dead thing is less powerful than its enemy, it can be.

"Go. Take your pet with you," my rescuer says.

I watch it all, then another pair of hands grabs me and spins me around. I ball up a fist and swing, just barely stopping my blow before it lands on Efram's face. Great, both the men I was just fantasizing about here with me now. Could my life get any more awkward?

"What was that? What did you say to it?" Efram demands, still gripping both my shoulders tight and shaking me.

"I don't know," I say, pulling out of his grasp.

"You won't be safe around here, now!"

"Well, great," I say. "What were my options? Let the

locusts run free? You know they would've killed everyone in the bunker."

"It would probably be best if we move her," pretty boy says.

"Who the hell are you?" I ask.

Anger makes me tense. He smiles and it makes my heart skip, even though it pisses me off at the same time.

"Rafe," he says, with a flourish and a bow.

Could he be anymore over the top? Or better yet, could I find it any less intriguing.

"Right," I say, trying to not be petulant.

The hairs on the back of my neck are standing on end. We're being watched. Almost like he realizes it at the same time, Efram grabs my arm and with long strides heads towards my bunk, Rafe following along.

"Were going to move you, now," he says.

He's moving fast enough that I need to run to keep up. "I'm not going anywhere without Rowan," I gasp.

"Don't be a fool," Efram says.

"Moving one of you is going to be hard enough," Rafe adds.

I dig my heels into the ground and jerk my arm free of Efram's grip. "I don't care," I say, hands on hips. "I won't go anywhere without her. There's no way I'm going to leave her behind."

Efram rolls his eyes, shaking his head. He opens his mouth to argue but notices Rowan peeking out the door of my bunk. He sighs and seems to collapse in on himself.

"Fine," he says. "We'll have to figure it out."

He and Rafe exchange a look. I know I'm pissing them off, but it doesn't change my satisfaction at having stood up to both of them. What kind of person would I be if I left my best friend behind?

Definitely not the person I imagine myself as. Not the

person I'm going to be. Somebody in this world has to be better and if it's comes down to me, then so be it.

Walking boldly ahead of them I pull the doors open, step inside, and give Rowan a big hug. I don't know what I've gotten us into but at least I know she'll face it with me.

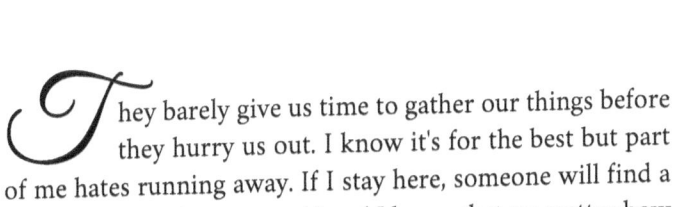

# CHAPTER SIX

*T*hey barely give us time to gather our things before they hurry us out. I know it's for the best but part of me hates running away. If I stay here, someone will find a way to use me. I'm not stupid and I know that no matter how tough I am, they would break me. The world is harsh.

"This is where we must part," Rafe says, holding my eyes with his when we stop at a door.

Efram is tense, watching with an unreadable expression.

"Okay," I say, unsure what else to do.

Rafe walks away and Efram opens the door, standing to one side and letting Rowan and I enter first. It's a room is much less sparse than ours was. Bookcases line the walls, filled with knickknacks and books and different things. He has a lush, full sized bed, complete with a comforter and a dozen pillows. Behind a curtain partition is a bunk bed. I have to wonder, does he share this with anyone?

"How do you afford all of this?" I ask.

Rowan nods, indicating that she also has the same question.

"People tend to mind their own business here," he says cryptically.

Kind of a dick comment but I guess people not asking questions of him is a good thing. Too many people saw what I did with the locusts, hopefully they won't come asking Efram. Course, I couldn't do anything to the undead puppetmaster though. Why didn't that deadie respond to my power? If Rafe hadn't intervened, I don't know what would've happened.

"You can use the bureau by the bunks. The curtain will give you enough privacy," Efram says.

"Thank you. How will we get our food tickets?"

"I'll ask for your reassignment after this all dies down and administration thinks it's just a rumor." He purses his lips and shakes his head. "You should've stayed in your room."

"And that woman, and how many more, would be dead!"

Something weird passes over his face. His eyes widen, his lips part, and then he smiles. It's like some mixture of admiration and surprise, but why would he feel that about me?

"Most people only think of themselves in survival situations," he responds.

"Some people don't."

"Clearly," he says. "I need to get a shower. Make yourselves at home."

He walks out of the room, leaving Rowan and I to settle in. We take our meager bag of belongings and sort them into the dresser Efram indicated we could use. Rowan climbs up on the top bunk and is out fast. I can't sleep so I get out a book, one of my most prized possessions, and read. Soon the door opens and Efram walks back in, hair wet and hanging loose, water dripping down across his bare chest.

My breath catches. He's ripped!

Ceremonial tattoos cover his glorious physique. In the world before, he could have been an underwear model. I've never seen a man built so well. And those tattoos. Something about them makes my blood buzz, different than what my power usually manifests as.

He's toweling his hair dry as he walks through the door, but when he stops and moves the cloth aside, our eyes meet and an instant connection springs to life. My belly does a little flip flop. I really have to quit thinking about these things.

"You're still awake? Get some sleep," he says with a half-smile, nodding to Rowan who is already dozing on the top bunk.

I swallow hard, trying to get the lump out of my throat. "Yeah, that's a good idea," I agree.

Taking my eyes off him feels like ripping two pieces of velcro apart. Even after I manage it, the image of him is still burned in my brain. Stepping behind the curtain, I pull it closed and lie down on the bottom bunk. I try desperately to find sleep but it eludes me.

There's something about the pattern of his tattoos that dominates my thoughts. Who am I kidding? There's something about him and I'm not stupid, I know exactly what it is. But now is not the time.

At some point I must fall asleep because I wake to the sound of voices.

"I've got a job for you," someone is saying. I recognize Rafe's voice.

"I can't take on a job, she can't be here alone," Efram replies.

"I'll stay," Rafe says.

"Watch her is all you had better do."

Is Efram threatening Rafe? Why?

"Me?" Rafe chuckles. "I'm the very picture of innocence."

"And I'm the last Herald," Efram snorts.

"You best be going," Rafe says. "You know how the dead don't like to be kept waiting."

"You're terrible," Efram says.

The door creaks open, the softly shuts with a snick. Then I catch the sounds of Rafe moving around and the chair scraping against the floor. I try to go back to sleep, but once more it eludes me.

"I can feel you're awake," Rafe says. "Brandy?"

Sitting up in bed and poking my head around the corner of the curtain, I ask, "You got alcohol?"

"We've got our hands in a lot of things here," he says with an insufferable grin.

I sit down across from him at the small table and he pours a drink for each of us in real glass tumblers. I don't think I've touched real glass like this since before my dad disappeared.

I down the shot in a single swallow. Holy crap that burns! I think I'll go a little easier on the hard stuff. I have no doubt Rafe would turn this into a full-on seduction if I let my guard down because I got drunk.

He leans in, elbows on the table. "So, how does a nice girl like you end up in a place like this?"

"You know it's not gonna happen, right?"

"What are you talking about?"

As charming as he is, as much as his voice is like soft fingers running across my skin, I'm not buying his innocent act. "Look, I like you, but let's take this a little bit slower."

"I'm still confused," he says, smile getting wider. "Perhaps you could take some time to clarify for me. What exactly are we talking about?"

"Don't act like you don't know."

"My dear," he says, placing a hand on top of mine on the table. "I assure you I am a complete gentleman."

"Funny words coming from a man like you" I say.

"Oh," he cries out placing a hand over his heart. "You wound me."

"I'm sure you'll survive," I say. In this exchange with him, I know I'm like the mouse being played with by the cat.

There's a fire in my lower belly, the attraction to Rafe is unnatural. It's too strong, too instantaneous. Right now, the best thing I can do is get away from him before I do something stupid.

"I'm going back to bed," I say, standing up and pulling my hand away from his.

The cold, underground air is un-welcome after the warmth of his touch. I imagine that warmth elsewhere and the heat spreads to my cheeks. Yep, really gotta go.

"Okay," he says. "You can rest safely knowing that I'm on duty."

"Thanks," I say. "Although I'm not sure it's outside trouble that I'm worried about."

"I won't bite. Unless you want me to."

I'd like to change my panties now, thank you.

Shaking my head, I step behind the curtain and pull it tight, trying to use the thin fabric to block him out. I toss and turn, having the most fitful night of sleep I've ever experienced. I keep waking up with fading dreams involving both Rafe and Efram.

THE SMELL OF BACON PULLS ME FROM SLEEP. THIS MUST BE the best dream ever. I don't want to open my eyes, but the smell is so strong that I have to look, knowing I'm going to be disappointed. Nobody could have bacon. I haven't even seen it in the luxury bins on rations day.

Groaning, I pull myself out of bed and stretch. The smell

doesn't go away so I step outside the curtain and see Efram working over the stove.

"Is that really bacon?"

He looks over his shoulder at me and smiles. "We do get our perks," he says. "Take a seat, breakfast is almost ready."

"You're a godsend!"

"Sent by something, surely..." he trails off.

I was joking but my remark made Efram go distant. I consider asking him about it, but before I can he's fixed our plates and set one in front of me. As he does, his sleeve rises and I notice his tattoos again. He sees me looking but doesn't say anything, just sits in the chair opposite of me and starts eating. Following suit, I put the bacon my mouth and it's like heaven. Crispy, crunchy, so full of fat and grease. I swear I could die right now and be happy. And then I take a mouthful of the eggs and literally drop my fork.

"These are real!" I exclaim.

Efram smiles, but before he can say anything there's a knock at the door. He rises from his chair and goes to answer it, but as soon as he does, Rafe steps into the room. He catches my eye over Efram's shoulder and winks.

"Dead guy in the second tunnel. Circumstances are real fucking mysterious," Rafe says to Efram.

He steps around Efram who seems to be pointedly blocking the way and moves closer to me. Rafe's stare causes a familiar surge of heat to flare across my skin.

"Glad to see you well," he smirks, his eyes drinking me in.

"Thanks to you," I say.

I notice a flicker of annoyance pass over Efram's features. "We can both go, I'll get Nathaniel and he can keep an eye here."

Rafe gives Efram a look, then turns and looks at me with pity on his face. "Oh, Nathaniel's a blast, I'm sure you'll love him," he says with obvious sarcasm.

Efram pulls his coat off the hook. "I'll be back in a second."

He steps out the door, leaving me alone with Rafe. The moment drags in to two and becomes awkward. I stare at my feet, having no idea what to say to a boy I think is cute. A boy who's not a boy at all and is probably way more experienced than me.

The curtain pulls aside with a rattle, saving me from the situation as Rowan steps out from our makeshift bedroom. Her eyes light up and her smile gets even bigger when she sees the plate of food waiting for her. She looks at me then rushes to the chair and sits down to start eating with a fury that makes me laugh. Rafe's eyes widen watching her wolf down the food and he chuckles.

"Hungry, I take it?"

Rowan glances up long enough to nod without pausing, shoveling more food into her mouth.

A moment later the door opens again and Efram comes back in with another man in tow.

"Aviella, this is Nathaniel," Efram says.

The newcomer has deep brown, soulful eyes, gorgeous dark hair and olive skin that begs to be touched. He wears a partial beard, neatly trimmed into tight lines that accent his strong jaw. The energy flowing from him is gigantic, but he seems intent to subdue it.

It's obvious that he's mysterious and special, like the rest of us but also different. I can feel his power caressing my skin, goosebumps run up and down my arms and I shiver. As if he can sense what's happening with me, his power pulls back. It's shocking and I stumble forward at the loss. Surprised, I look at his eyes and see no reaction whatsoever.

Feeling awkward again, I hold out a hand towards him which he looks at and then looks away without taking it.

Ouch. Nathaniel turns his attention to the door and looks around the room, pointedly ignoring me.

Ire rises at his actions. What the hell did I ever do to him? I don't even know this guy. What right does he have to treat me this way?

Or the better question is, what right do I have to care?

"I won't be long," Efram announces.

Rafe sidles over next to me, leaning in close like he's going to whisper something in my ear. "Don't you have too much fun," he says, obviously intending the whole room to hear.

Efram rolls his eyes and shakes his head. Nathaniel ignores us both.

Efram opens the door and he and Rafe leave. Nathaniel takes up his post next to the door, standing with arms crossed, staring at the floor. Sitting down at the table, I finish my breakfast but now it's lost most of its taste.

As much as I love Rowan she's not much of a conversationalist. We entertain ourselves the best we can, but I can't shake the awkwardness of Nathaniel in the room. His presence is dominating, constantly pulling on my attention.

"Do you play cards?" I ask, looking at Nathaniel.

He looks up, meeting my eyes for the first time since Efram left. Silently he walks over and pulls out a chair, taking place at the table. He reaches across and grabs the deck from in front of me, splitting it and shuffling it. He quickly deals each of us in.

"What are we playing?" I ask.

"Five card stud," he says.

"Okay," I say, looking over Rowan who shrugs.

We play five hands in quick succession. With each passing hand my suspicion grows that he's holding back. I keep studying him, wanting to know him better.

"How long have you been in this bunker?" I ask.

"A long time."

He keeps his eyes on the cards are the table, pointedly never making eye contact with me.

"Do you ever travel between the bunkers?"

"No," he says, dealing himself three more cards.

"Yeah, it's dangerous to travel," I say, feeling desperate to keep the conversation going.

Rowan grins at me, obviously knowing what I'm trying to do. I shrug and she wins the current hand. Nathaniel deals us in again and we start another round.

"So, what you think of the locusts?" I ask, immediately feeling like a fool.

Who likes locusts? I'm such a social idiot.

"They don't bother me."

That surprises me. "Really?"

He shakes his head in response. Okay then, not afraid of locusts, got it. He keeps losing the card game and I'm beginning to wonder if he doesn't just suck at it. At one point energy dances along my skin again and it hits me. It's him! He feels a connection to me too, he's just ignoring it. That son of a bitch. Now why does that make him even more attractive?

"Would you like some Nutri–Aid?" I ask, rising to make drinks.

"No," he says, shaking his head. "I don't trust the stuff."

"What's not to trust?"

Rowan stares with eyes wide, too. Who doesn't trust Nutri-Aid? It's one of the main staples of the apocalypse. It's not like you can drink the damn water.

He raises his head and meets my eyes. His dark, brooding stare makes me want to caress the angst off his face but he's so cold and distant. Power pulses in him, it's like a tide that he somehow keeps held inside. It's a feat, of that I'm sure. As our stare-down continues, I also realize it's not only his

71

power he's been holding back. He's been letting us win at cards too.

"You don't have to hold back," I say.

"I do," he assures me, cryptic and filled with double entendre. Well played.

Rowan glances back and forth between Nathaniel and I who still haven't broken eye contact. The door opening is what finally pulls us apart.

"I don't have time to be dealing with things like this anymore," Efram is saying.

"If you don't do your job, people will notice," Rafe counters.

"Let them," Efram says.

The two of them stop and stare at Nathaniel and me. It's clear from the looks on their faces that they can sense the tension. Efram clenches his jaw but Rafe smiles.

"Perhaps I was wrong," Rafe says, chuckling.

"Thanks for your help Nathaniel," Efram says. "But I think I can handle it now." He looks pointedly at Rafe when he says it.

Rafe opens his mouth like he's going to argue, but then changes his mind, smiling that devilish grin. "Of course," he says.

"I'll be around," Nathaniel says, rising from the table without another word. He doesn't even look at me as he walks out the door.

Efram stares at Rafe, like he's willing him to leave too. I'm getting a feel for Rafe so I'm certain that he stays just a bit longer only to annoy Efram.

"Do you have something to do?" Efram asks at last.

"Do I?" Rafe asks, his smile growing bigger.

"Yes, you do," Efram says through clenched teeth. "I'm quite sure of it."

"Oh, of course, you're right," Rafe says. He catches my eye

over Efram's shoulder and his eyes twinkle with delight. "I won't be far."

Rafe bows with a flourish of his arms and leaves. Efram sighs heavily and seems to finally relax.

"Now what we do?" I ask.

"How about some lunch?" Efram asks.

"Uh, sure," I agree. "But we just ate."

"Oh, right," Efram says. "Sorry. I'm not used to entertaining."

"Well, do you play cards?"

Efram smiles and takes the place Nathaniel just left. It's hard to keep track of time in the bunkers and it seems even harder here at Efram's place. He has nothing to mark it. No radio, no clocks, no timepieces of any kind. I don't know how many hours it is before there's a knock at the door. Efram answers and it's Rafe again.

"I thought we were done for the day," Efram says.

"Yeah," Rafe agrees. "But another one dropped. They need you."

"Nathaniel can't be here right now."

"Use magic, seal the door, that should keep her safe."

"I don't like it," Efram says.

"You do realize I'm not incapable right?" I ask.

Efram gives me a smoldering look that I'm not sure how to interpret. It's protective, hot, and annoying all at once. "Fine," he huffs. "Don't open the door, for anyone, for any reason. I don't care if you hear the final trumpet call, you stay inside. Do you understand?"

My hackles rise at the way he's treating me. I square my shoulders and grit my teeth. "Oh yes sir, thank you sir, without you I don't know how I ever would get by," I say in a false southern belle accent.

Rafe bursts out laughing while Efram rolls his eyes.

"You asked for that," Rafe says, still chuckling.

Rowan waves her finger in the air, giving Efram the 'oh honey you don't want none of this' without having to say a word. She makes me so happy. Efram has the decency to look at least mildly abashed. He mutters something, shakes his head, then goes out the door.

"Don't open it," he insists before leaving.

"Gah!" I exclaim after he's gone, turning to Rowan.

She shakes her head, smiles and shrugs. She grabs a piece of paper off a shelf and her magical hands fly through twisty motions I could never duplicate. In moments she's holding out a folded paper strongman. She dances it through the air between us, mocking Efram. She cowers before the paper to complete the scene and I can't hold back my laughter.

"You're the best," I tell her, pulling her into a tight hug. "Well, let's look around since we've nothing else to do."

Together we look over the shelves of stuff that Efram has collected. It's a lot of weird, eclectic things. I find a stack of old photographs but no one in them looks anything like Efram. There's a large collection of rocks, some have fossil imprints while others seem like nothing special. Another shelf has odds and ends from before the apocalypse. A broken cell phone, keys, credit cards with names on them that aren't his, and eyeglass frames with no lenses.

When I pick up a toy action figure to look at it, a book falls out from behind it and lands on the floor in front of me. Damn, I don't want to tear anything up. Glancing down, the book pulls all my attention. Its ancient, yellow-brown edges have water stains and what might be a real leather cover is bound by cord along its spine. On the cover is a symbol that pulses, expanding and contracting. I don't see it do anything with my eyes, it's in my head. Pounding. It's pounding in my thoughts.

Kneeling, I reach for it with a tentative hand, the hair on my arms rising. I'm detached, watching myself move towards the book like my body belongs to someone else. Tingles run up my fingers as I touch it, pulling the cover open. It's heavy, much too heavy for a book cover. It flips open and words run across the page. Literally run, like they're being poured onto it instead of written. They flow down until the page is full. It's a language I can't read but, in the middle, there's another symbol.

The pulsing grows louder. Suddenly it springs to life, reaching out of me without warning and the symbol comes to life. It lifts off the page, becoming bright red and glowing, twisting patterns in front of me. I fall into it. Fire burns through my body, charring my insides as it forces its way through me. My mind expands. I'm bigger than the room. Expanding bigger and bigger. Then I start being sucked into the symbol.

"What have you gotten into?" Efram shouts from some great distance.

His voice barely reaches me he's so far away, but the sound jerks me away from the symbol. I'm falling then I'm in his arms.

His perfect, strong, warm arms and he pulls me close against his chest. I can feel his power, like a comfortable blanket. I'm empty, drained, like there's barely anything of me left here. He is a rock I'm clinging to and barely holding on.

My body starts trembling. I want to make it stop but I can't. It's all I can do to hang on to that glimmer of me.

"Stay calm. You've activated something… you shouldn't have looked at those, damn it," he curses. "Those aren't for play. I told Rafe this was a bad idea."

Everything fades away.

## CHAPTER SEVEN

*E*verything becomes surreal. Efram carries me to the bed, lays me down and places a cover over me. Behind him, Rowan stands looking scared and worried. My moment of awareness fades and then blackness claims me.

WHEN I COME TO, KILLIAN, THE MAN FROM THE SUBWAY, IS standing and whispering with Efram beside the bed. I open my mouth to ask why he's here but immediately fade back out.

AWARENESS DIMLY RETURNS AND THIS TIME KILLIAN, EFRAM, and Luca are standing around, talking softly. Are all the guys from the subway here? Their voices are low and tense.

"What's happening to her?" Efram asks, his voice tight, jaw clenching, chopping off each word. "She should be awake by now."

"She's activated something," Killian says, shaking his head. "She shouldn't be alive.

Luca's aqua eyes stare at me with a deep sadness.

Efram throws his hands in the air, shaking his head. "Damn it, I knew I shouldn't have left her alone."

"Which book was it that she read?" Killian asks.

My head is spinning, darkness claws at me, calling me back. Struggling, I try to focus on the conversation, even though no one seems to realize I'm awake. I try to say something but my body isn't responding. Only then do I realize my eyes are still closed.

How am I seeing them?

Efram takes the book I looked at and hands it to Killian who looks over the pages, his frown deepening before his eyes go wide. "This is an initiation book!"

"You think I don't know that?"

Killian looks up from the book, still frowning. "Right," he says, shaking his head. "This book, it should have killed her. She's untrained and unprepared."

Well, leave it to me to be the cat curiosity almost killed.

Killian kneels next to the bed and presses a finger to my palm. An energy passes from him to me and my breath quickens. My eyes flutter open and my heart pounds in my chest. It roars, drowning out all other sound. My power races across my skin and I feel every motion in the room like it's touching a raw wound. I recoil from the overwhelming sensations and my body convulses on the bed.

Ronan pushes past the other two and kneels, his commanding eyes bore into my soul, a buoy in the storm that I desperately grasp on to. "Be calm. You're okay," he says.

My body submits to his voice and I know he's using the same ability to make my power submit as he did when I first met him. My heart rate slows and my breathing returns to normal. His eyes take on a faint glow and his energy flows out, surrounding me in warm light. My own energy responds, reaching out for his, intertwining and mingling. Pleasurable sensations race through me and out across my body along with a sense of well-being.

His eyes widen and his perfect, kissable lips purse tightly. Oh no! Don't worry, you're making me feel great, I want to say but I can't.

"Gavin," he says. "An energetic parasite got in, it's attacking her."

Gavin comes forward. They are all here! I try to sit up but immediately collapse again, unable to sustain my own body weight. There's a weakness in my muscles that I've never experienced before.

"You're fine," Gavin says, flashing me a gorgeous smile with a glimmer in his eyes.

I try to talk, opening my mouth, wanting to say something, anything really. No sounds come despite my best effort.

Gavin leans in, placing his hand six inches over me and moving it down from my head towards my toes. He moves his hand back up and stops over my heart. "Hmmm," he says, glancing over his shoulder at the other guys.

"How bad is it?" Killian asks.

"I need to handle it now," Gavin says.

"Do it."

"Wait--," Efram starts, but Gavin has already placed his hand on my heart.

I have barely a moment to register that Gavin has his palm on my breasts—that's hot— before the room goes distant.

～

EVERYTHING IS WHITE AND GLOWING. IT'S SO CLICHÉ IT'S sickening. Turning a slow circle, I find nothing but white all around. Okay then, what now?

"Hi, Aviella."

"Daddy?" I say, heart stopping as I turn to the sound of his voice.

"Yes baby."

I choke back a sob. All of a sudden I'm a nine year old little girl again, scared and needing her daddy. He smiles, holding his arms out and I rush into them.

He closes his arms around me, squeezing me tight against his chest. Nothing, nothing in the entire world could be better than this. Tears stream down my face and I don't care. The past ten years I've held out hope that I would see him again. Being in his arms is the fulfillment of every wish I've ever had.

"How?" I ask, not looking up from his chest.

I'm afraid to let go. Afraid that he'll disappear.

"You needed me," he says.

"Oh, daddy," I sob.

"I know," he says, stroking my hair. "It's okay. You don't have to be strong anymore."

Something niggles at the back of my thoughts. That doesn't sound like something he would say. It doesn't matter though, he's here.

"I've missed you so much," I say.

"I told you I'd come back."

"I know, daddy."

Straightening myself up, I wipe away my tears and look him up and down unable to keep the smile off my face. He looks haggard, worn, like he's been through hell but I don't care because he's here!

"You look like hell," I quip.

"It hasn't been easy," he says smiling.

"Where have you been?"

"Trying to get to you, of course," he says, grinning from ear to ear.

Something passes behind his eyes, I can't quite put a finger on it. I try to think about it but as soon as I do, a warm, glowing feeling fills me. I'm just so happy to see him.

"You've really grown up," he says.

"Yeah, I've made some new friends too."

"About that," he says, his face growing serious. "You can't trust them, Aviella."

"What you mean?"

"I mean quite simply that you cannot trust them. They're going to use you. Their only interest is in your power."

"No, daddy, it's not like that," I argue.

Doubt dances through my thoughts, weaving in and out of them. Something isn't right.

"I assure you it is," he says. "I've traveled through hell to get here to warn you."

He grimaces like he's in pain and for just an instant I see a wound on his chest that looks like it's bleeding black blood. It's gone almost as fast as I saw it, making me wonder if it was there at all.

"Daddy, what's going on?"

"I don't have very long," he says. "I'm having to fight them off just to be here with you. They want to use you. Don't trust them. You should try to escape, get away. Come to me."

"Come where?"

The whiteness around us shudders. It's weird and hard to describe, but it's like it blinks. When it does, my dad fades away and becomes a black outline for just an instant.

"I can't stay," he says, face grimacing in pain. "Just remember my words."

"No, daddy, you're wrong. I know these people. They're good people."

The whiteness around us blinks once more. This time there are distant voices, too far away to make out what they're saying, but someone is yelling in concern. It echoes around, bouncing off the empty whiteness surrounding my father and me.

"Damn it," he mutters.

Three open wounds appear on his chest, oozing black goo. He looks down and shakes his head. "That's all the time I have," he says. "Remember, Aviella. You can't trust them. You should run away."

The whiteness blinks and my head explodes with blinding pain. It's almost more than I can stand. I drop to my knees, hands flying my temples. It's like my mind is going to split apart.

"Daddy?" I whimper.

"I got it," Gavin's voice says.

The white fades and blackness claims me.

I STARTLE AWAKE, SUDDENLY AWARE OF BEING COMPLETELY drained and exhausted. Rowan's face appears, hovering over mine an instant after I open my eyes. Her smile spreads from ear to ear and she cups my face in her hands. Tears swell in the corners of her eyes. She holds me like that for second and I smile at her, feeling a bit shaky but better.

Rowan straightens up and mimes drinking something.

"Yes, please," I say.

She nods enthusiastically and turns, walking out of my sight, but quickly returns and hooks an arm under my shoulders, lifting me up. She holds a cup to my lips and helps me sip. The water is a true godsend.

"How long?" I ask.

Rowan lowers me back to the bed and sets the water glass aside without answering. She mimes food and I smile.

"Good try," I say. "But you're not getting out of my question that easily. How long was I out?"

"Three days," Efram says, appearing next to Rowan.

"Three days!"

"You're lucky to be alive," he says.

"Yeah, well that's me. Always getting into trouble."

"I'm serious," Efram says. "You just tampered with a mystical system that mages train for years to prepare for. And even then, they often don't survive it."

Mages huh? Is that what the guys from the subway are? "What can I say?" I quip, smiling. "I'm a special snowflake."

I look around the room hoping to see them. I have so many questions but they're nowhere in sight. Rowan notices me looking and shakes her head, giving a sidelong glance at Efram as she does. I know she's trying to warn me not to ask. I can only imagine there's some tension flaring there.

"You'll need to sleep more," Efram says. "Your body is going to need the rest."

"I wish I could disagree," I say, exhaustion weighing heavily on my limbs.

Rowan helps me eat and by the time I'm done I can barely keep my eyes open. She pulls the blanket up tight around my neck and I fade out.

I don't know how long this goes on. Every time I fall asleep it's like I'm traveling. I'm never aware of where I go, but I am very aware I'm going somewhere. It's weird. Every time I wake up Rowan is there. Sometimes Efram is as well and when he's not I can hear him moving around the room. She continues to feed me and bring me water and several times she even has a damp washcloth to wash my face.

Finally, one time I wake up and I don't feel exhausted. I start to sit up but Rowan stops me. She shakes her head, looking very stern, pressing me back down into the bed by my shoulders.

"I'm fine," I tell her.

"She places both hands on her hips and shakes her head, her long, curly hair bouncing around her face. I can't help but chuckle.

"Seriously Rowan, I'm fine."

"Let her get up," Efram says.

Rowan glares at him but steps aside. I rise to a sitting position and wait for the wave of dizziness to pass. When I open my eyes again and look at Efram and Rowan they're both surrounded by glowing colors. It's a ring around each of them that fluctuates like a strange rainbow. If I squint my eyes I can almost--.

"What are you doing?" Efram asks.

"I don't know," I say, honestly. "Trying to figure out these colors."

"Colors?"

"Yeah, you both have them. It's weird."

"You're seeing auras?" he asks in disbelief.

"Sure, whatever," I say, having no idea what he's talking about.

I'm a child of the apocalypse and I still don't understand half the crap that comes out of his mouth.

"That's impressive," he says. "And you couldn't do this before?"

"Nope," I say, shrugging.

Rowan watches the two of us like we're tennis players, batting a ball back and forth. She takes a seat next to me on the bed and puts an arm around my waist, holding me protectively. That's my girl.

"How are you feeling overall?" Efram asks.

"Fine, I was having weird dreams, but other than that I feel good."

"What you mean weird dreams?"

"I kept feeling like I was going somewhere but I could never quite put my finger on it. It was like I never actually arrived to where I wanted to be."

His brow furrows as he frowns. Shaking his head again, he bites his lower lip and then sights, shrugging. "You are completely unique."

"Uh, Thanks? What exactly does that mean?"

"It sounds like you're astral projecting."

"Oh, of course," I say, like that explains anything.

There's a knock at the door and before any of us can turn to answer, it swings open and Rafe comes walking in. The moment he steps over the threshold I pick up the scent coming from the bowl he's holding in his hands. My mouth is instantly watering and my stomach grumbles loud enough for everyone to hear.

"Hey, hey, hey," Rafe says with a mischievous grin. "I brought you the most kick ass recovery soup ever made."

"Oh my God," I say. "Whatever is in that bowl, I have to have it now."

"That's what all the ladies say," Rafe says, chuckling.

Out of the corner my eye, I catch Efram rolling his eyes. I decide to ignore it because after all, Rafe is just being Rafe. I stand and a wave of dizziness hits, but Rowan is right there to steady me. I lean on her and realize how lucky I am to have her as a friend. She helps me over to the table, pushing my chair in. Rafe places the bowl down and I inhale deeply, savoring the smells. When I put the first spoonful in my mouth, my taste buds explode with flavor.

"Oh my God!"

"You like it?" Rafe asks, his grin making it clear he knows the answer.

"I've never put anything better in my mouth."

"Well I've got other good things you--"

Efram clears his throat, interrupting what Rafe was about to say. The golden eyed man is completely unabashed as he watches me eat the soup. It takes all my willpower to not pick up the bowl and slurp it down. I want to take the time to savor it, enjoy it. It does seem to have some restorative properties. As I drink, warmth spreads throughout my limbs and I start to feel alive for the first time in days.

"I've got things to attend to," Rafe says. "I'm glad you enjoyed the soup."

I pick up the bowl and lick the last few drops from the edge. Then I stare at it, disappointed, wishing there was more.

"I'll walk you out," Efram says.

I pick up a pen and begin doodling on a blank piece of paper laying on the table. It's idle, something to fill the time. I'm trying to sort out all my feelings and my thoughts. I feel different. It's not anything I can put into words. It's a sensation, an awareness that's new and bizarre.

"Where have you seen this symbol?" Efram asks, staring intently at the paper.

Looking down, I realize I don't even know what I just drew. "I don't know."

He stares and his power scans over me, probing. "Try to remember," he says, coming closer and taking a seat beside me.

I do. He reaches over and takes my hand in his and a jolt passes between us. The hair on the back of my neck rises and suddenly I sense him, I know his emotions. Almost I know his thoughts. His violet eyes widen and he jerks his hand away.

"I feel you," I say staring into his eyes.

"I know," he says. "The question is, why?"

"Do you feel me?"

His energy pulls back as Efram stiffens, like he's struggling to control himself. I can feel it, like he's building a wall between us.

"You need to learn psychic defense," he says.

"Will you teach me?"

His brilliant eyes lock with mine, almost they seem amused, and they're certainly unwavering now. "Of course."

~

EFRAM BEGINS TEACHING ME HOW TO USE MY POWERS. Strangely enough, the exercises my dad did with me as a child are a very good groundwork for what I need to do now. It's all a matter of mental tricks to help me focus.

We pass through the next several weeks like a training montage from one of those old pre-apocalypse movies. Mostly it starts out with little parlor tricks. Rowan is my ever-faithful assistant as well as friend. She's quite often the target of my practice. If I focus on her, I can pick out things about her thoughts, feelings, or sometimes even her past.

It's kind of tricky, but I learn to focus not on her but kind of around her. Then I see the real Rowan beyond just her body. The colors that surround her, her aura, become brighter and then I just know things. I can sense her like she's a part of me.

"That's it," Efram says, encouragingly. "Keep focusing."

He's trying to teach me telekinesis. Furring my brow, I concentrate harder, willing my power to flow along the channel I'm imagining. The fork lying on the table in front of me vibrates, which is more than I've been able to get it to do so far. Supposedly I have telekinetic ability. Scratch that-- I know I have telekinetic ability. Apparently, that's what they call it whenever I lose my temper and things happen around me. Now I have to learn how to control it.

I focus harder, pouring all of my concentration into it, tension building inside my body as the buzz grows louder and louder. Distantly, Efram is talking but I can't make out his words over the sound of the buzz in my ears. My entire world becomes that fork. It consumes me. That fork will do what I want it to do. Suddenly, it rises off the table and shoots across the room like a bullet fired from a gun. The fork buries itself in the wall on the far side, resonating with force.

I feel drained, every ounce of energy I have is gone. I collapse into the chair gasping for air. My head is pounding as the buzz recedes, leaving me empty.

Rowan has crouched down beneath the table to avoid being hit. She peaks up and looks from me to the fork and back to me.

"Sorry," I pant. "I guess I don't really know my own power. Worse, I can't control it."

"That's exactly what you can't do," Efram says.

"What?"

"Doubt yourself," he says, placing a hand on top of mine.

The energy between us is a sharp jolt. My heart jumps into overtime, pounding in my chest, my breath is short now for an entirely different reason. I can feel him. His loss, there's something there. What is it? I want to know and instinctively I reach for him.

Efram gasps and jerks his hand off mine. He turns away, crossing the room, his back to me.

"Sorry," I say. "I can't help it."

"It's fine," Efram says, cryptically. He still doesn't turn around and look at me.

I can feel the emptiness, the ache inside of him. He's lost someone or something very dear to him. It calls to me. I want to help him. I want to heal that wound inside of him. For the first time in my entire life, being something other doesn't feel like a curse or a punishment but a true gift. I know I can help him.

Someone knocks on the door and Rowan bounces her way across the room to answer it. She looks out the door, shakes her head, and starts to close it.

"Who is it?" Efram asks.

Rowan looks over her shoulder, gives a half smile, and shrugs. Efram frowns and crosses to the door himself. When he pulls it open, a man in a suit is standing there. One of the dark suits favored by those who work for administration. He looks grim and serious, talking with Efram in a low, hushed voice so I can't make out their words. He hands Efram an envelope.

Efram opens it, his eyes scanning over the paper inside. He looks up at the man and nods his head. "Fine." Turning, he looks at me. "I want you to come along."

Rowan bounces with excitement and reaches for her shawl but Efram looks at her and shakes his head. "I'm afraid you wouldn't like this at all."

Rowan looks crestfallen and mimes wiping away tears from her eyes before squaring her shoulders and turning to go sit at the table and pull out cards.

"Sorry Row," I say.

I go over to her and give her a hug. She smiles and nods her appreciation. I get with Efram and we follow the man out into the tunnels of bunker E274.

After a time, we come to a door that requires a key code. The man we're following looks around before producing a key and punching in the code. He holds the door open while we step through and then pulls it shut behind us, making sure that it's locked again.

The new corridor he leads us through is cleaner and better lit than anything I've ever seen in the bunker. It's obvious we're going into a nicer area. He confidently leads us through a twisting maze of tunnels with various offshoots. Even only a little way in, I'm completely lost. I couldn't find my way back out of here if my life depended on it.

We turn another corner and enter a huge chamber. We're standing on a walkway that passes over a lake. It takes me a minute to figure it out, but the lake is growing rice. A handful of workers plod their way through the small plants. Interesting. This is the first time I've seen the systems used to feed the bunkers since the apocalypse and everyone went underground.

We cross over the lake and enter another set of tunnels that shoot off in all directions. Finally, we come to another door and the man leading us pulls out another key and enters yet another code. This time we step through into a room with comfortable chairs, couches, and small tables. The walls are lined with bookshelves filled with books, knickknacks and old artifacts. The space is criminally huge compared to the spaces normal people are afforded.

Efram doesn't seem surprised or taken aback at all. I do my best to take it in stride, like this isn't completely mind blowing. Our guide leads us through this room over to a door and stops, leans in close to Efram and whispering in his ear. Efram nods and the man opens the door, letting us through.

The room we step into is small with an overwhelming stench. I gag the moment I walk through. My stomach lurches and I clench my jaw tight, resisting the urge to vomit.

"Oh God, what is that smell?"

I should've looked first. The middle of the room is dominated by a steel table on top of which lies a bloated body. Efram doesn't seem to be affected as he walks straight up to the table. Stealing my nerves and trying to breathe only through my mouth, I walk up with him.

Efram's eyes take on a faint glow as he leans in and he

seems to grow bigger, like he fills the room more than he physically should.

"Wake up," Efram says, his voice incredibly low and gravelly.

The man jolts awake, he looks around, disoriented, but when he sees Efram he stiffens. The dead man shrinks back like he's terrified.

"Relax," Efram says, taking command.

Efram's voice is so different, it almost seems like something else has taken him over.

"Leave me alone," the body says, his voice gurgling like it's coming through water.

"You'll be moving on to another plane soon enough. Unburden your soul and tell me where the money is."

The dead man looks uncertain and then a rebellious gleam comes into his eyes and his mouth becomes a hard line. A pressure builds in my forehead. It doesn't hurt exactly but it's strange, a new sensation I haven't had before.

The room around me fades like I'm having a daydream that I'm not controlling. I see an image of a trunk floating across the room towards me. As the vision becomes clearer, I can tell that it's in the back end of a transit car. One of those big military vehicles they use to travel above ground. There's a red stripe spray-painted on the side.

"It's in a transit car, isn't it?" I ask.

Efram raises an eyebrow and the dead guy frowns.

"That bastard doesn't deserve it. He-- " The dead guy passes out, or rather he dies again.

"Killed him," I finish for him, meeting Efram's eyes.

Admiration beams from Efram and I feel a swelling of pride.

"You're certainly coming along. Keep that last premonition under your hat though."

Efram leads us out of the room and the man we followed

here is waiting outside the door. Efram takes a clipboard from the man and make several notes on it before handing it back.

"There you go," Efram says.

The man looks over the clipboard and nods. He reaches inside his suit jacket pocket and pulls out another envelope. Silently he hands it to Efram who tucks it away and then we're led back to our bunker.

I'm electrified by the new experience. I never knew I could do anything like this. It's thrilling, exciting, and almost a little bit overwhelming.

Once we're back in the safety of our bunk, I can't contain myself any longer.

"That was amazing!"

"You did very well," Efram says.

"Yeah, but what was that? How? Do you always? That guy was dead!"

Efram smiles at my babbling. Taking a deep breath, I push down my excitement and try to regain some semblance of composure.

"Better?" he, arching an eyebrow.

"What was that?"

"I'm a necroseer," he says.

I wait for him to say more but he doesn't.

"A necro-what?"

"A necroseer, I can talk to the dead," he says.

"Oh," I say, surprised. "Wow."

"Well it's not all roses and bouquets," he says. "But it pays the bills."

"It's amazing."

Efram simply nods, pulling out the envelope he was given. He opens it up and unfolds some papers and I can tell by his face he's surprised at what he reads.

"What is it?"

"We've been invited to a dinner party," he says. "Well, technically I have, but it says I can have a plus one."

"The admin has invited you to a dinner party?"

Rowan shakes her head violently side to side. She starts miming about how bad an idea this is.

"I know," Efram says, looking at Rowan. "There's almost nothing more dangerous than a dinner party among the upper crust."

"Sounds like a good time."

"You have no idea," he says.

Rowan begins miming trying to reinforce how bad an idea she thinks this is.

"I get it Rowan," I say, agreeing with her. "What can we really do? If Efram doesn't go it's going to look bad. I imagine that looking bad isn't going to be good for us either."

"You're right," Efram says. "We don't have a choice."

Rowan sighs, stamps a foot, and then nods her agreement. She begins miming furiously and Efram looks at me, obviously wondering what she's trying to say. I don't know why he can't see it, it's plain as day to me.

"She's coming too," I translate, a grin spreading across my face from ear to ear.

"Oh shit," Efram says, knowing better than to argue.

"So, how does one dress for a shindig like this? I've never gone swimming with sharks before."

CHAPTER EIGHT

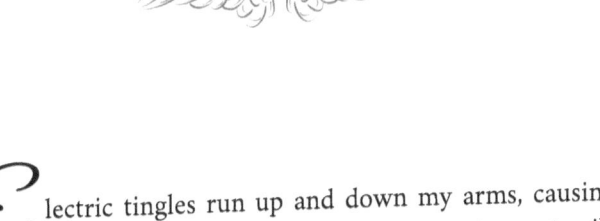

*E*lectric tingles run up and down my arms, causing the hairs to stand on end. Nervous excitement roils in my stomach as we approach the elite bunker. The door alone makes it obvious that we're entering a richer sector. It's in immaculate condition, not a hint of rust or scrape on the paint.

Two burly men in dark suits stand to either side. As if connected to each other, they turn their heads simultaneously and drill us with their gazes. Neither says a word as Efram walks right between them and up to the door. When he reaches for the wheel, the man on the left places his hand on Efram's arm to stop him.

"Allow me, sir."

"Thank you," Efram replies.

The man turns the well-oiled wheel and opens the door as sounds of conversation and music pour out around us. There's a light scent, something I can't quite put my finger on, that wafts along with it. It's nice and reminds me of better times.

We walk into the room and the butterflies in my stomach

go crazy. There are dozens and dozens of people here, all dressed immaculately. This is the bunker elite. Those who are rich and powerful enough to secure the best positions. I'm sure it's just me, but it seems like every eye in the room turns towards us when we enter. It's almost like I'm being sized up, a prize cow about to be offered for slaughter. Great, just the kind imagery I need.

Rowan takes my hand and squeezes it. Glancing over at her, she smiles reassuringly.

"Thanks," I whisper.

I've never been good in social situations and this is worse than anything I've ever experienced. The sidelong glances, the tone of conversation, the way they fall silent whenever we move anywhere near them. It's distressing, nerve-racking, and makes my stomach feel like it's tying itself into knots. I'm completely out of my element. Rowan, for her part, seems to be completely at ease. She smiles and nods and points at some of the people and their outlandish dresses.

A buzz breaks out across the room, growing louder. The crowd starts a round of soft applause. I look around, bewildered, trying to find the source of the excitement. It only takes a moment before my eyes land on the most outlandish man I've ever seen. He's gargantuan and dressed in the most garish outfit, a scarlet red, rhinestone encrusted suit. He has pasty white skin, thinning hair that's slicked back to his head, and beady eyes. Everyone has turned to greet him and he smiles, opens his arms wide, and does a half bow. I'm pretty sure that he could not bow any further without toppling himself over.

"Thank you, thank you," he says. Even his voice is smarmy.

"Thank you!" someone shouts from the crowd, which is greeted by laughter.

"Oh, you know I love you all," he says. "I appreciate you coming to my little gathering."

"Who is that?" I whisper, trying to catch Efram's attention.

"That's the admin," he says in a low voice.

"He looks like a pretentious douche."

Efram grimaces and places a finger over his lips, shaking his head side to side. "Watch what you say here," he says. "The walls have ears."

I look around quickly, for some reason I almost expect to see actual ears on the walls. I don't of course, thankfully. That would be creepy. Rowan catches my glance around and laughs silently.

I wasn't paying attention until it's too late. The admin is approaching us. He's making a beeline straight through the crowd that parts around him. They whisper at his passing and it makes my skin crawl. I don't want their attention and I sure as hell don't want the administrator's attention either.

"Efram!" the admin says, holding out two thick hands.

Efram reaches out and takes the admin's hand in his. Instead of a normal handshake the admin clasps both his fat hands around Efram's and shakes his entire arm in an exaggerated gesture.

"Most excellent work," the admin says. "I'm so glad you were able to accept my invitation to this little get together."

Little get together? There's more wealth being spent in this one room on the food and drink than what's spent on an entire month's rations for half the rest of the bunker. It's extravagant and ridiculous.

"And this must be your new protégé," he says, turning his attention to me.

As soon as his eyes land on me I wish I were in a shower. I frown and open my mouth, about to say something stupid, but Rowan kicks me in the shin. The admin is still standing in front of me, his hand extended, obviously expecting me to take it. I look from his hand to his beady little eyes and the throbbing of my shin pushes me to be polite.

"Pleased to meet you," I say, instead of what I was thinking.

"Yes, I'm sure it is," he says. "I hear you have quite a bit of promise."

How has someone as important as the admin heard anything about me?

Rowan nods enthusiastically, lending her support to his words. The fixed smile on the admin's face falters as his beady eyes dart over to my friend. He clears his throat and something passes across his face that I can't quite read. All I know is, I don't like this guy. His garish outfit, his grand gestures, and his false humility all rub me the wrong way. If I'm swimming with sharks, he's their king. I know, deep in my bones, that his only claim to leadership is that he happened to have enough money to buy it. I doubt he has any real skills and he certainly has no care for those under his rule.

He recovers himself and avoids looking further at Rowan, focusing on me instead. His clammy hands clasped on mine are making it impossible for me to suppress a shudder.

"Let me show you to the serving tables," he says. "I'm sure there'll be something there to your liking."

Thankfully he finally releases my hand. I wipe it on my pants and Rowan mimes her surprise and shock, like I just committed the greatest faux pas. Efram clears his throat, trying to call the two of us back in line. We follow the admin through the crowd which parts easily around him. No matter how much they try to hide it, it's obvious all eyes are on us.

"Please make yourselves at home," he says. "This spread is but a small token of my appreciation for your work. You've done such an excellent job for me so far, I very much look forward to hiring you again in the near future."

My stomach does a flip and another wave of nausea grips me. The admin is the one who killed the dead guy from earlier, he just all but admitted it! And he wants to hire us to do it again? What am I getting myself into? I don't work for murderers.

The admin is smiling at me brightly and I try to smile back but I can't. I have to say something. "You are—"

Rowan kicks me in the shin at the same time that Efram grabs my arm and squeezes my bicep tightly.

The admin stands, waiting for me to finish my sentence. I snap my mouth shut, choking down the words I was going to say, but I'm unable to come up with anything to fill the silence. He continues waiting and the tension in the room grows.

I should just say what I'm thinking, what are they going to do?

Bad things. Really, really bad things.

"So incredibly gracious," I finish, putting a fixed smile on my face.

"You are so kind," the admin says. "I have to attend my other guests but please enjoy yourselves. If you need anything at all just let me know."

"Oh, I will."

Deep in my bones the buzz waits, ready to come to my command. Luckily, with Efram's help, I have more control of it now or this would've been an entirely different scene.

The admin nods and takes his leave. Rowan turns towards her, cups my face in her hands and kisses my forehead. I know she's concerned and that helps.

"That was too close," Efram says. "Remember, low-profile. Don't draw attention."

"I'm trying," I say. "But that guy is a—"

Efram places his hand over my mouth, cutting me off again. "No," he says. "Don't even think it."

A waiter carrying a tray of drinks passes by and Efram's eyes land on it. He steps around me and grabs three glasses off the tray. He hands one to me and one to Rowan. It's filled with a purple-ish liquid. Efram sniffs his while swirling it so I duplicate the motion, unsure what the hell I'm doing. Watching him, he sips it slowly so I follow suit. There's a sweet explosion of something slightly fruity with a hint of an oaky flavor that bursts across my tongue. Almost instantly it feels like my nerves relax. This is good.

"What is this?"

"Wine," Efram says, arching an eyebrow.

"Hmm, I like wine," I say, grinning.

Rowan bounces from foot to foot and mimes walking into a weaving, circular stance. I don't understand what she's trying to tell me this time. I look over at Efram to see if he gets it.

"She's telling you not to drink too much," Efram says. "Just enough to take the edge off."

"Why?"

"Wine can have strong effects," he says.

I nod understanding that I don't really have. Turning back towards the crowd, I let my eyes scan over them, barely aware of the fact that I'm also using my power. Only after my work with Efram do I recognize what I've always done instinctively. As I do, I sense something familiar, hot, enticing.

The feeling draws me in and following it to its source, I spot Rafe. He's making his way through the crowd, carrying two glasses with his insufferable grin.

"Aviella," Rafe says, stepping up and handing me a fresh glass.

"Rafe!"

The wine is helping, I feel much more relaxed than I have since we came here.

"I didn't think you were going to be here," Efram says.

Rafe hasn't looked away and for a moment that seems absolutely timeless, he and I are intimately connected. I flush hotly, unable to look away, but then he turns his attention to Efram and the moment is broken. Only then do I realize I've been holding my breath. Damn it girl, keep a lid on it.

"I hear you saved the day, again," Rafe says.

"I had help," Efram replies.

Rafe's brow rises. "Promising student."

"She's more than that," Efram says, and there's something cryptic and heavy about his words.

"Of course," Rafe says, his brilliant smile flashing and making my heart sore. "She's obviously very special."

He meets my gaze again and this time his energy presses against me, almost like it's his body on mine. It leaves me dizzy, breathless, and out of sorts. Desperate for some way to cover myself and feel less exposed, I drain the glass of wine in my hand. Even with breaking eye contact, Rafe's energy lingers, a fever on my skin. He's insufferably hot. Dangerous.

His energy emboldens me, like his presence is waking something wild inside of me. Something rattling its cage and ready to break free. I can't help but think how great it would be to just let go. Let my power run free, to stand before the world as me, not hiding, not ashamed ever again.

My head has a light, buzzing feeling to it. My entire body is buzzing. Interesting.

"I need more wine," I say, maybe a little too loudly. A pair of extravagantly dressed women look down their noses and sniff.

Efram steps over to the bar and when he returns it's with a glass full of clear liquid. I sip it, immediately disappointed that it's plain water.

"I asked for wine, not water!"

This time more than a few heads turn my direction.

"Low-key, Aviella," Efram warns.

"Let her live a little," Rafe says, his voice caressing my skin and my thoughts, coaxing me.

"You know that's not a good idea," Efram counters.

Rafe's energy tingles across me and through me at the same time. Intriguing, enticing, it calls to my power. "Efram," he says. "She's not a child, let her live. What can it hurt?"

Rafe grins and I see the devil dancing in his ruby eyes. I want to impress him, but more than that I want to live. Dammit I should go to do what I want to do! All my life I've been hiding, holding back, never able to just let myself be. How bad could it be if I just do what I want?

Rafe's eyes bore into me, burning with a gold-red intensity, igniting fires across my skin.

"Rafe..." Efram trails off.

I want a glass of wine. What's so wrong with that? I like the way it makes me feel, light and relaxed. It makes me feel good. The wildness coursing through my blood agrees and my power surges unexpectedly.

"I don't want water!" That time everyone in the room heard me and turns to look at the commotion.

Rowan gasps as the water in my wine glass boils and then there's a loud pop. The liquid in my glass is no longer clear, but a beautiful rich purple.

Oh shit, what have I done?

Everyone's eyes are on me. The room has gone completely silent.

Fear rises in my stomach sending cold chills through my limbs. Rafe forgotten, I look past him at all the people staring. Some with their mouths open, but most with cold, calculating looks. Evaluating how they could use the situation to their advantage. Use me.

My glass slips from numb fingers, crashing to the ground and sending a bouquet of purple wine spiraling across the floor. The sound of it breaks the silence and as if on cue, there's a collective gasp.

I'm in trouble.

"Time to go," Efram says, grabbing me by the arm.

"Probably for the best," Rafe agrees.

Rowan slaps Rafe on the arm, shaking her head and waggling a finger at him. Rafe shrugs and laughs. "How was I supposed to know?" he chuckles.

Efram drags me towards the door but it's obvious that my secret is out. They may not know what all I can do, but they know I have powers. I really screwed this up.

Efram pulls me towards the door and I stumble along behind him listlessly. Rowan maintains her grip on my other arm which keeps me from falling. I take one quick glance over my shoulder and immediately regret it. The admin stands in the middle of the crowd like a king holding court. His beady eyes focused on me. There's no doubt he knows I have powers nor is there any doubt in my mind that he intends to use me. Knowing already what he's capable of, a cold shiver to run down my spine.

As we step outside the door, Rafe and Efram argue about what to do next. I just blew our cover in the biggest way possible and I don't even know how I did it. The buzz of their conversation rings in my ears long after the door closes behind us.

# CHAPTER NINE

*W*e move through the tunnels of the bunker in silence. I can feel the tension radiating off Efram and even Rafe seems subdued. Rowan puts an arm around my shoulders and is running her hand up and down my arm reassuringly. I'm lightheaded and kind of dizzy, which I assume is a side effect of the wine.

I can't believe I did that. I mean on one hand, wow, it's super cool. If I'd done it when it wasn't going to possibly get every one of us killed, that'd be even cooler. Good to know nothing much has changed. I'm still socially awkward and quite capable of drawing the wrong kind of attention to myself.

Rafe and Efram both keep looking over their shoulders like they're expecting to be followed. The tunnels of the bunker are a maze and I'm quickly lost. We come to a crossroads and Rafe pulls up short.

Efram pauses and looks at him. "What?"

"I need to go check on some things," Rafe says, making himself as clear as mud.

"Sure," Efram says.

I can't read the necroseer, so I'm not sure if his 'sure' is actual agreement or more of an 'of course what else what I expect of you' comment.

Rafe is unfazed, his slow, sardonic smile unperturbed. He leans in close to me and it's almost annoying that I can't catch my breath. "I'll be back soon," he whispers. "Don't do anything I would do." He steps back with a wider grin, spins on his heel, and takes off down a side corridor.

Efram harrumph's, grips my hand and pulls me back into motion. His long strides make it so that I have to almost run to keep up. My lightheadedness isn't helping. I stumble more than once but thankfully Rowan is there to keep me upright.

Eventually I start to recognize the tunnels we're moving through. As they become more and more familiar I realize we're close to Efram's place. We turn one last corner and I know at last exactly where we are. It also helps that Nathaniel is standing outside the door.

Efram stiffens. Nathaniel looks ridiculously handsome. Is there some kind of rule about the apocalypse that every man I meet has to be an absolute hottie? I mean, talk about lucky, right?

Nathaniel turns towards us, stiff as ever, and waits for us to close the distance between them. "Efram," he says, his voice sober.

"Have you heard already?"

"Heard what?"

"Good," Efram replies. He keys the door open and steps aside, motioning for Rowan and me to go in. I stumble stepping over the threshold and once more Rowan saves my life.

"Sorry," I giggle.

I don't have any idea what's funny about this, but it really is.

"I'll be right in," Efram says, smiling in a way that I'm sure is meant to be reassuring but only reminds me of how badly I screwed up.

Rowan helps me to a chair and once I'm settled she stands, staring longingly at the closed door. There's a bit of a glow on her face, a happiness that I haven't seen before, a reverence even. I'm not sure what it is and obviously I'm too buzzed to think it through, so I let it go.

"I'm not sure I feel so good," I observe, as my stomach flip-flops.

My statement pulls Rowan's attention. She frowns, places her hand on my forehead, then shakes her head. She moves around me and goes into the small kitchen and begins fixing a couple of drinks. It suddenly hits me how badly I've screwed up. I should have had better control. That display was not only foolish it was childish. I was being silly.

My dad would be so disappointed.

I've imperiled all of us. The danger we're in is real. I have to realize it's not just me anymore. In the orphanage when I lost control it hurt nobody but me. But now these other people depend on me. I can't let anything happen to them.

I could blame Rafe, sure. He egged me on, teased me, but that's how he is, what else should I expect? Who am I to blame him for my actions? The worst part is, I feel like I let Efram down. The idea of the necroseer being disappointed in me bothers me a lot. I don't know what we're going to do. As long as we're in this bunker we're going to be in danger. Because of my actions we're probably going to have to leave. Then we'll be running into God knows what.

I was so excited about how amazing and cool my power can be that I lost sight of how dangerous it is. I can't let anyone know what I can do. Dammit, I'm a fool.

It was easier when I thought my gifts were just a curse that could only be used to destroy. Now that I can actually do something constructive and good with it, it makes me want to use it more. I want to see what I can do. Damn myself and my curiosity. I've never been this way before.

It makes me wonder though why only some people have talents.

It doesn't seem fair that some get powers but most don't. I have to wonder what makes me so special? Ever since I opened that book, I've wanted to study more. I want to learn, but not on my own. I need a guide, a teacher. I promise myself I won't mess around like this again. I will never put anyone else in danger. I know with help I can learn to control this better.

Rowan sets a glass of Nutri-aid in front of me and I sip it gratefully. My head is still spinning, and I feel kind of light and giggly, but the nutrient drink helps push the nausea away. Plus I'm more sober than I was.

I've come to realize that I just have to be patient. Besides, I've got other mysteries to solve. I know what Efram is now but what about Rafe or Nathaniel? And are Ronan, Killian, Gavin and Luca the mages Efram mentioned? What am I?

# CHAPTER TEN
## EFRAM

"We have to get her out of here," I say.

"What happened?" Nathaniel asks.

"The admin knows about her abilities."

Nathaniel's eyes glow and I can sense his anger rising. His jaw tightens and he shakes his head. "How?"

"You wouldn't believe me if I told you."

"Try me," he replies.

Along with his anger I perceive his grace. His aura is edging towards blinding white. Damn angels, they're such a pain in the ass.

"Okay, how about water into wine?" I say.

"You're kidding me," Nathaniel says, gritting his teeth tightly.

"At a time like this, the last thing in the world I'm doing is kidding you," I say, trying to keep irritation out of my voice and failing.

"All right, we have to get her out," he says, like it was his damn idea.

Angels are dicks.

"I can arrange transportation," Nathaniel says. "It's going

to take me a while though."

"Yeah, we're going to need it," I say. "By the way, Rafe was there to."

Nathaniel doesn't have to say a word, his anger and frustration are palpable. I'm surprised he doesn't go full on angel and bring his wings out. He and Rafe barely get along but why should they? One's a demon and one's an angel. They're natural enemies.

"Did he have anything to do with this?"

"No," I lie.

No point in starting a war right now. I'm going to need both of them—well she's going to need both of them. What is it about her?

"Fine," he says, shaking his head. "I'll get something ready by the morning."

"I hope we have that long," I say. "The admin himself took a particular interest in the display."

Nathaniel sighs. "Fine. Keep her safe until I get back."

He walks off without another word.

"Hey," I yell after him before he can turn the corner. "Why were you here?"

"It doesn't matter now," Nathaniel says looking over his shoulder. "She's all that matters."

He disappears around the corner, leaving me with that little mystery. It's fine, I'll file it away with all the other ones. Besides, he's right. There is something about her. She's different, powerful, but it's not just that. She's like a magnet drawing me in. Her energy calls to me, I want to meld with her, join with her in ways I've never joined with another. It's strange, exhilarating, and frightening all at once. There's no way she should have this kind of power over me.

I also know that her power is only going to grow stronger. She's barely starting to scratch the surface of what she's going to be able to do. I have to help her learn to control it.

I shouldn't have taken her to that dinner. It would've been better to piss off the admin than to put her in that situation. I push aside all my doubts and reservations as I unlock the door and step inside. I can't let her see me weak and Rowan in particular is incredibly perceptive.

"Okay ladies," I say. "It's time to start packing. We're going to have to travel light so only bring the essentials."

Aviella is resting her head on the table and Rowan is brushing her hair. Aviella looks up, eyes blurry, and groans. The effects of the alcohol must be wearing off.

"I'm so sorry, Aviella says, her eyes bleary. "This is all my fault."

"It's not your fault."

"I should've kept it under control."

"It doesn't matter," I say. "We have to start packing, now."

"But you'll have to leave all your stuff behind!" Aviella says.

I smile trying to be reassuring. "It's only stuff, we'll get more where we're going. Besides, I've been wanting to leave for a while. Now, pack."

Aviella stands and she and Rowan go and begin packing their meager belongings. I set about the task of finding what I want to take and what I need to leave behind. I select several tomes, a couple of puzzles, doing my best to make sure I also pack light. I don't know that I'll ever be back here again, but that's fine.

Once we're finished it's a matter of waiting. The three of us sit at the table and I can tell the girls are nervous. They keep shifting, making and breaking eye contact, and looking around the room like they're lost. I pull out a deck of cards and shuffle them.

"Care for a game, ladies?" I ask, smiling big.

# CHAPTER ELEVEN
## NATHANIEL

*I* know divine blood when I sense it and Aviella definitely has it. It's been my duty since the Dawn of Time to ensure the safety of those who carry the legacy. Their blood calls to me just like hers does. But there's a strength to hers, something more, something special.

In those with the gift lies the only hope this planet has of rising from the ashes of the apocalypse. The smells of unwashed bodies, stale beer, and urine assault my senses as I step into the rundown bar. It's not a nice place but it serves my purposes.

I work my way through the unusually crowded floor to the bar. Catching the bartender's eye, I order a club soda. He snorts, shaking his head, but fills it without another word. Hunching over my glass, I try to draw myself in smaller, I don't want people here to be aware of what I am.

A thin, mousy man slides into the bar stool next to me. He doesn't look over as he takes out a pack of cigarettes, places one in his mouth, closes the pack and then takes the one out of his mouth without lighting it.

"Bartender!" Humphrey calls. "Whiskey, neat."

Humphrey puts the cigarette back in his mouth and then takes it out again, still without lighting it. We've known each other for a long time and have worked together often. He's reliable, or at least as reliable as a human can be.

"I'm going to need to arrange a ride," I say without looking at him.

"How soon?" he asks, staring straight ahead.

"Now."

"Shit," Humphrey says. "You've got her!"

Every muscle in my body tenses in a low, cold rage. I pointedly don't look at him.

"What you know?" I ask.

"I don't know much," he says. "Only that the admin put a price on her head. A big one."

"Why does he care so much?"

"He summoned something," Humphrey whispers. He looks around, making sure that we're still alone. The noise of the bar is enough to drown out our soft conversation but that doesn't mean someone isn't using magical abilities to listen in. In order to make sure, I mutter a small phrase, blocking anyone from eavesdropping. Humphrey hears it, grimaces, and then nods.

"It's safe now," I say.

"The admin's gotten some scrolls," Humphrey says, shaking his head. "Or so I hear. Some kind of really dark shit. He's making deals with shadow powers. Word on the street is, he's looking to trade her for something this thing is looking for."

"Shit."

"Will surely hit the fan," he says.

"I'm going to need that ride, sooner rather than later," I say.

Humphrey nods, downs his drink and slams it on the bar,

motioning for the bartender to refill it. He places the unlit cigarette in his mouth, purses his lips, then takes it out again.

"Sure," Humphrey agrees. "I won't even charge extra. I can't go into agreement with whatever that bastard has cooking up."

"Good," I say, rising from the bar stool.

Sometimes humanity still impresses me. They haven't all forgotten the grace that is inherent in their nature.

I shouldn't be surprised what the admin is doing. Time has ground to a halt and there will eventually be a shift. Powers like Aviella's, her bunkmate's, and the other innocents that I've been trying to protect are crucial to what happens next. The new world depends on them. They are the only hope we have.

I must work fast. Everything is worse than I thought. If the admin has some shadow power, it's only a matter of time before this bunker falls. I have to have her clear of it before that happens.

Outside the bar, I burst into a run.

# CHAPTER TWELVE
## RAFE

I probably shouldn't have pushed her so hard. Sometimes I can't help myself and besides, it was funny. As it stands, as much as I hate to admit it, Efram is right. She's more than a mere student. My shadow sense tells me she's going to have a profound effect on all our destinies. I have to help make sure nothing sideways happens to her first.

Something is coming. I can sense it, crawling out of the shadows, rising up from below. The lower hierarchies have told me it's coming, the same demons I refused to align with once my pre-apocalyptic tasks became effectively null and void. I know how to handle most of them and I can still pull in a favor or two if I choose. I will if I have to protect Aviella. One way another, she will be all right.

Right now, I just need to gather information. How bad was the fuck up? How much attention have we drawn? It is the admin willing to make a move?

These are the things I need to find out before I go back. I'm more at home in some parts of the bunker than others. There are parts that, by my very nature, I blend into. Areas that Efram can't go and that Nathaniel would never make it out of. Being a demon has its perks.

The sound of roaring cheers echoes off the walls as I enter the lower level tunnels. Crudely cut from the stone, these tunnels aren't commonly traveled by the upper class. A few rough types pass me by but no one gives me a second glance. They know better than to mess with me.

Another round of cheers is almost deafening when I step into a large, open the chamber. The crowds are pressing up against a makeshift cage in the middle of the area. Cheap beer and ale flow freely, filling the air with the sweet scent of degradation. In the cage, two men are busily beating the hell out of each other. The crowd screams, getting more excited as more blood flows.

I move closer to group surrounding a lesser demon. He's taking their bets and making sure that the house still comes out ahead. I find it hard to believe nobody knows these fights are fixed. I don't think they want to know.

"Rafe!" Sal says upon seeing me.

"What's the word?"

"Shit is hitting the fan," he says, shaking his head.

"What do you mean?"

He frowns, looks at the crowd around us, then shakes his head again. I move in, picking up on his desire to not be heard. He leans in close enough that I can smell the garlic on his breath.

"Shadows are coming man," he whispers. "Bad stuff, way way down."

"Any word on who's summoning them?" I ask.

"No," he says. "And honestly, I'm not sure I'd tell you if I did know. I don't want to be involved."

I let my power caress him, pushing past his skin, driving into his core. He shudders, blinking rapidly and cold sweat breaks out on his forehead.

"You sure you don't know anything?" I ask, smiling.

"Damn it Rafe," he hisses, grimacing.

"Sal, we're friends," I encourage, my words echoing my powers of persuasion.

His eyes roll up into his head as he fights against my control. He clenches his teeth so tight I think he might actually break them.

"Rafe," he pleads, but still doesn't tell me anything.

He really doesn't know anything. If he did he'd have broken. Sal isn't known for his strength of will.

"Fine," I say, releasing him.

He wipes the sweat from his brow and glares at me. "I hate it when you do that."

I shrug and smile. I'd apologize but I wouldn't mean it, so what difference does it make?

"I'll see you around Sal," I say, watching him straighten himself up and square his shoulders like he might suddenly be brave.

Chuckling to myself, I turn my back on him in a display of utter contempt and walk away. Sal is way too far down the pecking order for me to be concerned, but I am going to have to look elsewhere for the information I want. Someone is calling the shadows and someone down here knows who it is. I need that information. Everything depends on it.

I make my rounds through the lower levels, heading towards what I know will be my best bet. Everyone I run into is whispering. Down here, among the dregs of society, they can feel it coming. That means it's big, really big.

The worst part is, I'm certain that it has everything to do with Aviella. Even without her little display of power things have been shifting. Letting her power slip is just going to accelerate what's already in motion.

"Let me in," I say, smiling as I place a hand on the shoulder of the big burly man guarding the door.

"You know they don't want you in there Rafe," he says.

"It was only a misunderstanding, let me go straighten it out," I say, pushing power into my words.

If they were smart, they'd hire somebody with better mental shields. As it is, their goon shakes his head side to side, trying to resist for about two seconds before he nods his head. Not only does he step aside, he opens the door for me. I walk in without making a scene.

Several tables are set up around the cramped space, each one crowded around by bleary-eyed poker players. I mingle among the onlookers, those without the backing or the balls to actually sit and play at these high-stakes tables. Here I'll find the information I need. If it's to be known, someone in this room knows it.

"What is he doing here?" a gravelly voice asks.

"Jack, haven't you given up those cigarettes yet?" I ask. "You know they're going to kill you, right?"

He coughs then places an oxygen mask over his face, breathing loudly. "You're not welcome here," he wheezes.

"Jack, that's no way to treat an old friend," I smile, moving through the crowd to stand next to him.

The eyes of the other players are on us, watching and judging. None of them are brave enough to move or get involved.

"Not... My... Friend," Jack coughs, accenting each word.

I place a comforting hand on his shoulder, leaning in to give us some semblance of privacy. "Tell me who is somebody in the shadows," I whisper close by his ear.

"He shakes his head and I push my power into him, caressing his essence, stoking the rage in his soul.

"Don't," he coughs, his face turning purple as he tries to resist my influence.

I'm much too powerful for that. He knows it, it's just part

of the game we play. As my power takes hold his resistance fades.

"You're so screwed," he says, coughing again.

"Just tell me who."

A grin forms on his feeble face, dark and malicious. "The admin," he says, chuckling until another round of coughing cuts in.

Shit. I have to get to Efram. Now.

# CHAPTER THIRTEEN

*L*ying in the bottom bunk, I pretend to sleep. Mostly I listen to Rowan breathing above me. I can't get my thoughts to quit circling around how badly I've screwed everything up. You'd think by now I'd be used to it, I've been an outcast all my life and none of the kids at the orphanage ever let me forget it.

I don't know how long I lay and stare at the mattress over my head. It seems like forever. I can't shake off the creeping sensation that something bad is coming. Even when I do sleep I have such weird dreams.

I toss on my side, listening to the mattress creak, half hoping that I wake up Rowan so I'm not alone. It's not just the boredom that's bothering me, I'm lonely. Which is stupid because my friends are right here. It's hard to believe what lengths they've gone to for me. They believe I'm special, but I know I'm just a weirdo, an outcast, someone different from everybody else.

There's a loud noise outside the door to the bunker and I jump up in bed cracking my head on the bunk above.

"Ow!" I exclaim.

Efram is already up and running for the door. I swing my feet off the bed onto the floor, taking a moment to hold my head. There's a small knot forming where I hit it. Rowan drops down off her bunk and sits next to me, pushing my hand aside and looking at my head. Then she leans in and places a kiss right on it.

"I know, I know, I'm a klutz," I say.

She smiles and nods her head.

"You don't have to agree with me," I laugh. Even when she's being sarcastic, Rowan makes me feel better.

Efram has stepped outside the door, leaving it partly open. Voices drift in, I recognize both Rafe and Nathaniel's. Sharing a quick glance with Rowan, we rise as one and sneak our way towards the door so we can eavesdrop.

"We have to leave here now," Nathaniel says.

"That's exactly what I was coming here to tell you," Rafe adds.

"I don't need your help, demon" Nathaniel says, his voice tight and low.

Rowan shivers next to me and I glance over. She looks scared and I can't blame her. Rafe is a demon?

The voices outside pull my attention back.

"Well that's too bad Nathaniel, because you do need my help and you're getting it, like it or not," Rafe says.

"The day I need a demon, Nathaniel growls. "Is the day I turn in my wings."

Wings? Is he saying he has wings? There's no way we've been hanging with a demon and an angel and been clueless about both. Why are they in the human bunkers?

"I think you'd look cute without wings," Rafe quips.

"Gentlemen, there's a time and a place," Efram jumps in.

I try to see what's happening, peeking out the crack in the door, but Efram's position blocks my view of the other two men. I wonder if he did that on purpose. His stiff body posture makes it clear that nobody is coming in the room until they've come to an accord.

"Fine," Nathaniel says.

"I've got no problem," Rafe says.

Efram stands, holding his position for a long moment before turning towards the door. As soon as he starts to move, I hustle back to my bunk with Rowan in tow. Doing my best to look innocent, I watch as the three men enter the room.

Nathaniel's energy beats against my skin with raw power. It's primal and my own energy responds, buzzing through my blood, the sound of it filling my ears. My heart rate soars through the roof. He has perfect lips, I wonder what they taste like?

Swallowing hard, I push aside all those crazy thoughts and reign my power in, something I never would have managed before working with Efram. Nathaniel doesn't even seem to notice. He keeps glancing sidelong at Rafe and it's clear there's personal history between the two of them.

"We have to move," Nathaniel says.

"With fire on her heels," Rafe chimes in, obviously trying to rattle Nathaniel who glares angrily.

"A perhaps overly apt description," Nathaniel grimaces.

Rafe glances at me with a wicked smile, "I do pride myself on being a cunning linguist."

Rowan gasps and Nathaniel growls in response.

Familiar heat pools in my belly and spreads, making my cheeks flame red. He always has this effect on me, damn him.

"They're coming for you, tonight. And they've got help you are not prepared for," Nathaniel says, overriding Rafe's racy comments.

"She's getting a handle on her gifts," Efram offers.

"Practicing on the nasty bunch that is coming for her is unnecessary and overkill for someone still learning. There

119

are underused routes we can use to get out. We must move quickly, before they get here. If we stay, it will get publicly nasty and make it even harder to escape," Nathaniel says.

The three men look at each other like they have their own private form of communication which I'm completely cut out of. As one they nod.

"We're already packed," Efram says.

He grabs his bag and Rowan I take the hint, picking up our own. Nathaniel leads the way out and we follow in uneasy silence along the more populated corridors. I can't help but notice the glances as we move through the crowded tunnels. They try to make it not obvious, but they're failing miserably. There's no doubt everyone knows something is happening.

Great, look what I've created. Go me.

Nathaniel moves us along quickly, with a certainty and confidence. No one tries to stop us for which I'm thankful. We walk through the tunnels until the crowd start to thin and then we come to a locked gate. Nathaniel produces a key and unlocks the massive padlock. When he opens the door it screeches loudly, echoing down the hallways. Instinctively I look around, expecting someone or something to respond to the sound.

"Hurry on," Nathaniel says, motioning us through. He closes the gate behind us and replaces the lock.

"Where are we?" I ask.

"We're in the subtunnels," Nathaniel answers.

My stomach ties itself into knots. There's something about this area that feels off. Nothing I can put my finger on, but more of a quiet, creeping nervousness, almost like I'm being watched. Nathaniel continues to set a fast pace through the empty passageways. They angle down, going deeper into the earth. It's not long before I'm sure we're at least one, maybe two levels below the normal bunker levels.

As we approach a flickering torch, there's a sound echoing towards us. It's a weird, shuffling, papery sound. I keep looking around, trying to find the source, but it's impossible. With the way the sound moves off the stone walls I can't tell where it's coming from.

Rowan grabs my hand and grips it tight in fear. Squeezing her hand, I smile reassuringly.

Rafe clears his throat behind us as he taps me on the shoulder. He motions for me to step to one side then slides in front of me. He moves up and stands beside Nathaniel, keeping pace with his long strides.

When we turn the corner, the source of the sound is almost right in front of us and the sense of dread that's been growing explodes. A small army of undead creatures are shuffling their way down the hall. The buzz in my blood rises, my heart pounds, and I'm breathing in ragged gasps. I want to lash out and destroy the unnatural to get rid of this feeling.

Before I can do anything, Rafe motions with his hands. His eyes flash from gold to burning crimson and I can feel him straining as his energy surrounds us. It's like a warm, cozy blanket, that you want to curl up in and take a nap. It makes my power recede and allows me to stay in control. I sense it's straining his abilities and see the grimace on his face. Gratitude blossoms in my heart, mixing with fear as I watch the procession work its way mindlessly forward. I notice that they all have a symbol I've seen before. A brand.

It's the one from my nightmares! What in the fresh hell?

I focus on it and a pressure increases between my brows, growing until I'm forced to look away. Rafe watches me, shaking his head in admonishment. He must've stopped me from looking at the symbol. That's probably a good thing considering what happened with Efram's book. Now certainly isn't the time to be knocked on my ass for three days.

Fear exudes from my belly making my blood run cold. The wrongness of watching the dead things shuffle makes my skin crawl. I can barely stand to be here. Part of me wants to scream, part of me wants to run, part of me wants to destroy them. I'm struggling to control my fear and the only thing that helps is the fact that I can't reveal our position. It's my fault we're in this mess in the first place. I sure as hell don't want to make it worse by doing something else stupid.

My power rises, but this time it's easier to take control. I push it down, not letting it go, knowing its unpredictable nature. I don't know how long we stand still, but at last the ghoulish, decaying creatures are gone and the corridor is clear.

Nathaniel leads us deeper, turning several more corners before we come to what appears to be a blank wall. He draws a faintly glowing sigil, which opens a passage and he waves us through. When Rafe steps up to the entrance he looks at Nathaniel, arching an eyebrow. Nathaniel grimaces, but nods and Rafe steps through without a problem.

I'm really going to have to ask him about the demon thing at some point when we're all safe.

We emerge onto a balcony that overlooks an open floor plan. The walls are covered in pale, glowing sigils and I can sense that there's some kind of protective energy coming from them. I look at Rafe who seems to be nonplussed. He isn't being affected by the sigils at all, which must mean he's not an enemy to Nathaniel. If Rafe had any harmful intentions it wouldn't matter that Nathaniel invited him in, the protective magic would've put up a resistance to his presence.

That puts me at ease. I barely know Rafe, but I can tell he's a good man. I hope Nathaniel can come to understand that too. I guess I shouldn't call him a man, he is a demon after all.

Efram has one of his books open and is quickly flipping through the pages. He glances up at the symbols and then back down. I know that he's trying to figure out how the magic in here works. His aura is glowing brightly as he studies, it's obvious he's doing what he enjoys.

Stairs on either side of the balcony lead down into a living room area below. Nathaniel takes the stairs to the left and I follow. His home looks like a sanctuary, a retreat from the world, almost a museum. He has the largest collection of exotic stuff I've ever seen. Having nothing better to do for the moment, I browse the shelves. Rowan falls in beside me, picking up various objects and looking them over. My eyes land on a canteen. My heart starts to pound in my chest, it feels like I'm falling, the room spins around me and I can't catch my breath.

Rowan drops the item in her hands and leans in, cupping my face and staring deep into my eyes. She shakes her head, begging me to tell her what's wrong with her pleading look.

I shake my head and pull myself free, turning to Nathaniel, "where did you get that?"

He looks over to the canteen I'm pointing at and blinks. The corner of his eyes wrinkle in confusion. "What?"

The angel is acting confused but he's also subduing his energy, pulling back from me and trying to shield himself so that I can't read him.

The canteen," I say. "It belongs to my father."

"In my travels," he says, shrugging and turning away from my gaze.

His aura is completely shielded now, I sense nothing. Why would Nathaniel intentionally veil his energy? What does he know that he's not telling me? I swallow and take a deep breath, trying to relax and not let random suspicion overwhelm me. Picking up the canteen and flipping it over, on the bottom I see exactly what I expected. Dad's initials are carved into the steel band.

"Nathaniel," I call. "These are my father's initials. Exactly where he carved them."

"People leave belongings behind," Nathaniel says, still not meeting my gaze.

"Do you know where he is? Where did you find this?"

"I've been a lot of places -- some are better left in the past."

"What does that mean?" I ask, anger rising.

"Exactly what I said," the angel replies.

His response has energetic punctuation to it. Rafe makes his way towards me, pushing his persuasive influence on me to let it go, but I'm not gonna back down. Not yet, I have to have answers.

"Did he give it to you?" I ask.

"No. There'll be plenty of time to reminisce on the past later, I really need to focus on these transit maps," Nathaniel says, turning his back on me.

My power rises, straining at the bonds I placed on it. Every fiber of me wants to interrogate him. Push him, make him tell me. My insides are on fire, I have to know.

Rafe places a hand on my arm. He wants to me to drop it, and lord help me the suggestion seems like a good one. Why shouldn't I just agree and move on?

No! I won't be manipulated. Jerking my shoulder away, I glare at the angel. "Nathaniel!" I cry, but the angel ignores me.

Rafe's power caresses across me. Like a lover's touch on my skin, too close, too much. He takes my shoulders in his hands and a warmth spreads through me. The demon is being far gentler than he ever has before, his energy isn't a fiery blaze this time but a soothing bath. He takes the canteen out of my hands and places it back on the shelf. My fingers are numb and I can't will myself to resist. Rafe's golden eyes hold nothing but sincerity.

"He's a puzzle. Angelics typically are. Given time, you'll find your father. I'm sure I can help with that, love." He lifts one hand to my face and caresses my cheek with a thumb.

I deflate, too tired to resist the demon's persuasion or push the angel any farther. I turn my face slightly into Rafe's hand, lifting my own and briefly touching his before pulling away and turning to the rest of our group.

Rowan and Nathaniel are locked in a silent contest of wills. Communicating in some unspoken way.

"What do you suppose those two are chatting about?" Rafe asks playfully.

I can't keep my sour mood. It fades away and I let it go. I feel a certainty that Rafe is right, I will find my father again. With the help of my friends.

Looking up at him, I have to consider that maybe demons have gotten a bad rap.

He glances at me with a thoughtful look on his face and a half smile. "I'm not just a demon," he says, his voice soft like he read my mind. Maybe he did. "I'm a neutral ancient, not some shadow puppet groveling before an unfeeling master. I've never hurt an innocent person– quite the opposite actually."

The truth of his words sings in my blood. He's not lying.

"I'm sorry," I say, apologizing for my doubts.

"It's okay," he assures me with a wink. "I've got infernally thick-skin."

I can't help but laugh.

"We can't stay here," Nathaniel speaks up. "I'll have to go in and see about getting the transportation arranged. This place will only be safe for so long."

"I wouldn't expect anything less," Efram says. "If they've

got undead armies wandering the lower levels, it won't be long before this bunker falls."

The necroseer gazes at me and my sick feeling returns. I'm going to be the cause of the fall of this entire bunker. Great, another thing to pile on my conscience.

## CHAPTER FOURTEEN

ours pass without much happening. Nathaniel comes and goes, looking grim each time he shows up. He and Efram often confer together, leaving Rowan and I on our own. Rafe realizes we're bored after a while and comes over.

"You ladies look like you need something to do."

"I want to help," I say.

I can't stand the waiting. My stomach is roiling and my heart feels like it's beating in slow motion, pressing against a heavy weight. All I can think about is how I wish time would speed up. But then again, I don't want it to go faster because I know bad things are coming. There's no escape, no relief from this sensation of building dread.

"I understand," Rafe says. "How about something to pass the time?"

"I brought some puzzles," Efram says from across the room.

"Perfect!"

Rowan and I exchange a look, and she shrugs. Anything to take my mind off what's coming.

Rafe digs through Efram's bag and pulls out a puzzle, laying it on the table before us. It's a one-thousand piece, pretty mountain scene. Dimly I recall when I was really young seeing something similar and a wave of nostalgia passes. I'm thinking about my dad again. I couldn't have been more than two or three when we were in the mountains. He taught me a lot up there even though I was so young. I don't know very many three-year-olds who could set a trap but I could.

We dump the pieces out and start building the puzzle. Rowan and I work together and the time passes, still slow, but at least it doesn't feel like it's crawling.

Rafe and Efram are going over the maps of the transit system for the bunker. They're debating what's the best path to get us out of here. I wish I could help. I don't know anything about reading maps like that though.

"Our best bet is going to be to make a break for the main line of the subway system," Efram says, pointing at the map and tracing a line with his finger.

"But we won't be able to use the cars, they're too heavily guarded. We'll have to travel on foot."

"We can try to steal a car," Efram counters.

"That could work, but-- "

They continue debating and I tune them out.

"Anybody hungry?" Efram asks and as if on cue, my stomach grumbles and I realize I am hungry.

Efram must have heard it because he smiles and goes into the small kitchenette.

I return my attention to building the puzzle. Were about halfway there and the picture is starting to come together. The closer it comes to completion, the more it brings back memories of my dad. I know he's out there somewhere. I would feel it if he was gone. I'm certain of it.

Whatever Efram's cooking smells great. The scent of it

fills the room and my mouth starts to water. He carries two plates over to the table and sets them down for Rowan and me. Two burritos lie on each and I've never been so hungry. Rowan grabs hers up and wolfs down the first one down before I can even pick one up. I laugh and she smiles, shrugging and patting her belly, nodding enthusiastically.

"I take it was good?" I ask.

Rowan continues to nod and I laugh again. I eat my burritos and she's right, they're delicious. It's the kind of food we couldn't afford, not having the credits to buy anything this fancy.

Once I'm finished eating, I'm tired. I don't know what time it is. Nathaniel doesn't seem to believe in keeping timepieces.

"We should probably all get some rest," Efram says.

I nod my agreement and look over at the sleeping area. There's not a lot of room, Nathaniel obviously isn't used to entertaining. He has a single large bed and that's it. My stomach sinks at the thought of having to sleep on the floor when there's a nice comfy bed, but I'm also not willing to let my friends sleep on the floor either.

Efram looks at the bed single bed as well and then looks at me. I see the fire in his eyes as well as feel it in his energy.

"I'll take the floor," he says, in complete opposition to what I sense is really going on inside him.

"No," I say. "Please, let's just share it."

"Don't worry about me," Rafe says. "I'll stand guard while you guys rest."

I give Rafe a grateful smile and Efram reluctantly nods his agreement. Efram, Rowan, and I go to the bed. Rowan climbs in first, and then Efram, and I sleep on the outside edge. It doesn't take long before sleep claims me. For the first time since I've left the orphanage, I don't have any strange dreams. Nothing frightening or disorienting happens. I sleep like a baby, the most peaceful and restful sleep I've had in recent memory.

"Wake up, Aviella."

I wake with my head resting on Efram's chest. He has a hand on my head and my leg is thrown over his. I'm pressed against him and the realization makes me groan in embarrassment. I start to pull away but his grip tightens.

"Shhh," he whispers.

"What is it?"

I become aware of my surroundings and the illusion of peace is gone, drowned out by the sounds of locusts and groaning undead.

Efram sits straight up in the bed, alert and ready. Rowan is also awake and all of us have our eyes on the door to Nathaniel's place. It takes several long, tense minutes for the sounds of evil outside to pass us by.

I let go of a breath I didn't realize I was holding.

"That was close," Rafe says. Sweat is pouring down his face and he looks pale.

"Are you okay?" I ask, jumping out of the bed and going over to him.

"I'm fine," he says. "It came a little faster than I was ready for, I expended a little extra effort in hiding us."

"I need to learn to do that," I say. "I'm sure I can help."

"I'm sure you could."

Before anyone says anything else, the door swings open and we all jump. I'm ashamed to admit I yelp. My cheeks flush, hoping no one noticed.

Nathaniel steps into the room with six young people in tow. Two girls and four boys. They all looked scared, confused, and every one of them pulses with power that makes them feel energetically similar to Rowan.

Nathaniel ushers them in and seals the door behind them. They stand huddled together waiting for direction.

"We'll be leaving soon," Nathaniel says. "Make yourselves at home until then."

"Are we safe?" the youngest girl asked, she can't be more than thirteen or fourteen.

"For now," Nathaniel says.

He strides across his apartment and starts packing. Efram is also packing his bag and Rafe is moving around, putting things together as well. Rowan has already packed our bags so we're ready to go. The newcomers stay close to each other, not coming very far into the room. I see them casting sidelong glances at me, but for the most part I decide to ignore them for now.

The dread in my stomach and the feeling that something is about to happen keeps mounting. It's making the hairs on my arm stand up. I'm not sure what to expect but I know it's going to be bad. The room takes on an air of dread as well. Everyone's mood is somber, quiet, more subdued than ever. We're about to do something either incredibly stupid or incredibly brave. It's a toss of the dice which way it's going to go.

Rafe walks out into the middle of the room, holds his arms out either side and spins a slow circle, laughing. Everyone stops what they're doing and watches the demon. Once all eyes are on him, he stops turning, flourishes, and takes a bow.

"They're not indomitable folks," Rafe says. He speaks with such confidence it stabs into the dread, deflating it. "Everyone here is going to make it to the railcar, okay?"

"The tunnels are overrun with locust and undead. The admin is walking with them and they don't do anything to him," a young man from the new group says.

"Shut up Marco," the other girl says, and the boy hangs his head.

"The admin is a fool if he thinks he can control the dead,

they get hungry and his spells won't last." Rafe says.

"All of that's true Rafe," Efram says, his eyes on me with obvious concern. "But there's still a price on Aviella. She's a big target."

Rafe shrugs like the admin's magic is only a minor crimp in his plans. He smiles and looks at each person in the room. When his eyes land on me, his energy pours into me, bolstering my spirits.

"So, I'll veil her," he offers.

"You have enough energy to do that and veil us?" Efram asks.

"You'd be surprised what I'm capable of, Efram, but today you're going to veil us. Aviella is a top priority," Rafe says.

"No need to convince me of that," Efram responds flatly.

"It's settled. I'll veil Aviella, you'll be on the group, and Nathaniel can handle the undead," Rafe says, grinning broadly.

Nathaniel gives Rafe an annoy glance but says nothing.

"I'm fighting to," I chime in stubbornly, not letting their attempts to render me useless slide.

The newcomers look surprised and my friends look resigned. I can tell they don't want to rile me up out of fear I might lose control of my power and bring the bad things down on us too soon. I understand that, but I have to learn how to fight. If I'm going to have this much power I'd better be able to use it.

The three men look at each other and seemingly come to a consensus.

"Basic training is ordered then. We can spare some time for that, we have to actually," Rafe says, speaking first.

A flood of relief passes over me. I was worried they would try to fight me. I know I'm right. I have to learn how to fight so I'm glad that they see it my way. Rafe takes charge, ordering Rowan and I, plus the newcomers, over and he begins coaching us. It requires concentration, which I'm having difficulty with. Every time Rafe comes close, I can feel his power caressing my skin. It makes me feverish and distracted.

He coaches us into being able to call up the power and channel it. I find this rather easy. Once he explains it, I'm surprised I never figured it out on my own before. It starts out the same as it always has with a low buzz deep in my bones, but now I can actually pull it towards my center and then channel it out along where I want it to go.

"Now focus," Rafe says. "Pull the fire into yourself, ride it like a wave, you're going to use it and channel it. Imagine it, burning away your existence. The fire is between you and everything looking at you. That is the veil."

I concentrate like he says. Pulling my energy in, it is like a fire roaring to life, burning through my veins. Trying to focus it and make myself disappear is trickier. I put all my mental energy into it and I almost get it, but then Rafe steps in close. Power leaps out of me, surrounding him, and his own mingles with it. I want to just melt into him. I know I should pull back but I don't want to. He feels too good. A shudder runs down my spine and pleasure floods through my senses like a huge hit of dopamine dumping into my brain. There's a quality to his energy mingling with mine. It's deepening the connection between the two of us.

"No, not yet," Rafe says, pulling himself back.

My power flares higher, hotter, reaching new heights. It's fueled by my desire! I didn't realize that before. As I look back over my life and all the times I've lost control, I understand that every time there was something I desired-- my power, it, responded. Usually it was a desire to get away from danger.

"She's got it," Efram says.

His words pull me out of my own inner monologue and I

look around, seeing the looks of surprise on everyone's faces. Looking down at myself, I don't see anything different though.

"Yes, she does," Rafe says with pride.

"I knew she would be a fast study," Efram says.

"Let it down now, Aviella," Rafe says.

I'm not sure exactly what he means, but I just make the decision to let go and that seems to do the trick because the other students gasp like something amazing just happened. Rafe claps his hands in a long, slow clap. It's not a mocking sound at all, and it fills me with a sense of pride.

He leans in so close that his mouth is next to my ear. His hot breath warms my skin and his power is like a gentle caress.

"Let your fire flood you," he whispers. "Focus on your desire."

I swallow hard, trying to suppress a shiver. He stares into my eyes and I want nothing more than to taste his lips. He moves his hands up and down my arms without actually touching me, causing the energy between the two of us to behave in strange and subtle ways. Desire threatens to over-take me. It's something I've always suppressed. Being an outcast, being different, didn't make for easy relationships. I've never dated a boy, hell I've never even kissed a boy.

"Take hold of it, use it," he says, his voice husky.

Focusing on his words and pulling on the energy, I center it, making it a part of me. Suddenly it hits me. My power is a tool of survival not something to repress. The moment I realize that, everything shifts. I grab onto the energy and ride it like a wave. It's exhilarating! I'm carried away with it, alive in a way I've never been before.

I motion with my hands and with a wave, I focus a blast in front of me. Power hits Rafe, pushing him back three feet. Lifting my hand palm up, I raise him off the floor. He starts laughing and that's how far I can carry my concentration. I lose control and the energy bleeds away, letting him drop to the ground.

"Perfect," he says.

"Holy..." one of the new boy says.

"And that, children," Rafe says, climbing to his feet, "is how it's done. Now the rest of you slackers, practice."

Nathaniel walks over, his face grim as always, and stands in front of me. The differences between the angel and demon are palpable. Rafe is passion, heat and recklessness. In contrast, Nathaniel is the controlled eye of the storm, a vortex of leashed power.

He has a small stone bowl in his hands, filled with some kind of a liquid and a brush. "May I?" he asks.

"Sure?" I make it a question, unsure exactly what he's planning to do.

Nathaniel dips the brush in the liquid, taps off the excess, then draws a symbol on my face. It tingles as he completes it and then my blood starts to sing. I can feel the connection between the two of us now even stronger. I realize that Nathaniel reflects a piece of me, my stubborn, unbending side. I touch the angel's arm and he stops, looking down into my eyes. For a moment his stoic defenses are down and I see him in all his divine glory. His power, so carefully constrained, is unleashed in that brief instant.

I call on my own power, channeling it through his and he shudders. His body is so close to mine and with our energies entwined, tension forms between my thighs. I know he feels it too, he bites his lips and closes his eyes, clenching a fist.

But then with a groan, he forcibly separates his essence from mine, shaking his head and stepping back. I open my mouth to say something but he moves on to Rowan, painting the same design on her. A feeling of disappointment floods me but I know at some point I'll break through to him.

Efram takes front and center. He has a book in his hand, which isn't surprising at all, and goes over it before he looks up and clears his throat.

"The main threat we're going to face out there is undead," Efram says. "The thing to remember is that they're pretty much brain-dead. They're corpses with only the basic functions. What you have to also realize is that the shadow forces using them are not brain-dead. Do not alert them to your presence. If they don't pick up anything with one of their five basic senses then they have nothing to transmit to their masters telepathically. The goal out there isn't to run at them. It's to slip past. The protective veils will help, but the rest is very necessary common sense,"

"Don't make unnecessary noise. Don't broadcast your fear with panic. Panic has a scent. Go in knowing you're going to slip past them into the railcar." Nathaniel says.

"Failing that, run like hell. Only fight if you must, the goal is to get out of here. We're not doing the hero thing today-- that would be suicide," Rafe chimes in.

Everyone exchanges an emotionally charged look. Fear plays along my skin and I swallow hard. This is it, a run for our lives.

# CHAPTER FIFTEEN

*A*s soon as we step out into the tunnels, the sense of despair is unmistakable. It's like a layer that lies over the entire bunker. Still, there's nothing to indicate the danger that we know is present, only an eerie silence that has fallen across everything. Nathaniel leads the way and we fall into a ragtag group behind him, Efram and Rafe bringing up the rear. The angel moves quickly through the rough-cut tunnels, coming to a door which he lays his hand on and a sigil glows. He mutters something under his breath that I can't catch and the symbol glows brighter, then the door creaks open on its own. As if on some mystical cue, the echoing sound of locust wings fills the tunnel, doubling over on itself, making it impossible to tell where they are.

Nathaniel looks behind us and grimaces. "We have to run," he says. "Now."

It doesn't take more encouraging than that. We burst into a run, following the angel, who starts to glow as he runs. I realize I'm seeing his aura. But instead of shifting colors, it's moving towards a more steady, golden light edged in white.

The sound of locust wings grows louder and underneath

that there's a low groaning, moaning sound that sends chills down my spine. Nathaniel glances over his shoulder and shakes his head.

"Keep running," he says, then stops and steps over to the wall, running his hands over it.

Sigils appear where his hands pass. I want to stop and study them, but I know better than to wait. I keep running but spare a glance back over my shoulder. Nathaniel's sigils are sealing off the tunnel behind us. It may not stop whatever is coming, but it should at least slow it down.

Putting my attention forward, I focus on running. Ahead, there's a fork in the tunnel. I don't know which way to go, so I make a guess and head for the right. It splits off and goes a few hundred feet before it makes a sharp turn to the right again. I'm about to reach it when the ground rumbles and a shuffling sound ahead makes my blood run cold.

I try to stop, but I'm running so fast I skid on some loose gravel. I slide around the corner and come face-to-face with an undead patrol. The stench of dead flesh assaults my nostrils. I'm facing what was once probably a successful businessman. He's wearing a ratty, dirty suit but his face has mostly rotted off, leaving raw, glistening muscle and revealing his lower jaw. His teeth snap open and closed but it's his dead eyes that hold my attention. They're empty of any signs of life.

Instinctively, I slam down a veil like Rafe showed me. The dead thing's gaze passes over me without registering anything. He and the other five corpses with him turn and continue shuffling down the tunnel. Rowan skids to a stop next to me and the other six aren't far behind. All of them gasp seeing the undead and I have to pull harder on my attention to focus and keep the veil in place to hide us. Nathaniel shows up a moment later, grabs my arm and pulls me back. He leads the group back to the fork in the tunnel and takes us down the left path without a word.

My heart finally slows in my chest. That was close. I almost got us all killed.

I don't know how much longer we run because my time sense is completely skewed. Eventually we come to the end of the tunnel and there's a light ahead, growing brighter, then we pile out onto the platform. Two sets of rail tracks lie in front of it with a railcar on the far side. This one is different than the railcars I've previously seen. It's obvious this one is designed for going outside because it has enclosed cars. While the platform itself is empty, the power car, complete with shackled slaves, is still in place. I've never seen one of the trains designed for transfer between bunkers. The slaves are lying around on the car, seemingly unaware of their surroundings. My stomach sinks and my heart grows heavy as we gather in a group on the platform. Everyone is looking around, wide-eyed, uncertain, and scared.

"Were almost there," Nathaniel says, pointing at the car. "All we have to do is get over there."

"Nathaniel," I say, my voice quivering as I point to our left.

A large group of undead emerges out of a tunnel and onto the platform. They mill about mindlessly, not seeing us yet. There are so many of them. We're not ready to fight this many. It's too much.

Nathaniel sees them and turns back to the group, silently using hand signals. He indicates we should make our way across the platform and to the train. It's our only hope to get out of here. We start forward and Rafe's veil seems to be holding. The undead continue milling about without taking noticing of us. It's going so well until somebody makes a noise. One of the newcomers hits a pile of pebbles which skid across the concrete of the platform. We stop, frozen in place. There's a long moment that seems to stretch into a miniature eternity. I'm looking at the undead army and they're looking at me. No doubt about it, we're screwed.

There's a thunderclap and rising behind the undead army is a swarm of locusts. The clatter of their wings drowns out all other sound on the platform. They swarm over the undead, heading straight for us. The swarm slams into one of the support pillars and it crumbles, causing part of the ceiling to collapse.

They're only a few feet away, I have to do something. My power hums through my blood, the buzz of it drowning out the locust wings. It's now or never so I step forward, open my arms wide, and ancient words flow out of me, loud and commanding.

All my power pours into those words, leaving me drained and empty. It hits the locusts and they disperse, no longer a swarm. Several locusts drop to the ground, buzzing, and the rest fly around aimlessly like moths blinded by a bright light.

My head spins and my body feels too heavy to hold up. I've got nothing left. Efram catches me before I hit the ground.

I stopped locusts but now the undead are coming. While struggling to capture my breath and leaning on Efram for support another horror happens. Walking through the middle of the undead comes the admin himself. Still dressed in his bright scarlet outfit, his eyes burn with a deep-seated hatred. The undead follow his orders, moving along with him. Incantations leave his mouth and writhing forms take shape in the air. He's calling upon shadow powers, summoning things even worse than the undead.

Nathaniel steps forward, glowing with a brilliant, almost blinding white light. He calls forth words of power in a deep, booming voice and the writhing smoke-forms the admin's incantations were summoning dissolve in a puff of smoke. The admin glares at Nathaniel and I sense him reaching deeper, pulling on depths and reserves of power no man should have.

The enormous man spouts new incantations, pouring more force into his words. The smoke-forms take shape faster, becoming darker as they coalesce into solid forms. Nathaniel glows brighter and makes a slashing motion with his hands, like a knife cutting through the smoke and the shapes dissipate at his command. While the angel battles the admin, the rest of the undead are closing with us. The sense of danger heightens. I've got to get my breath back. I feel so weak.

Struggling with everything I have, I force myself to get back on my feet. Efram supports me by holding on to my shoulders for which I'm grateful. I waver for only a moment longer before I step free.

"Thank you," I say.

The undead are even closer, they'll be on us in seconds. The others are trying to fight, applying their powers the best they can, but none of us are ready for this.

Efram steps up beside me and growls. "Disperse," he orders, pointing at the undead army.

The amount of raw power he pours into that command is stunning, it tingles across my skin and settles low in my belly. My connection to him throbs with energy. His command disrupts the control the admin has over the undead, causing them to lose focus and slow their approach.

Rafe steps up to my other side and digs deep, pouring more power into his veil. His effort is palpable through our bond. I lend him what power I can, but I don't have much to spare. It's enough. His shields strengthen and it keeps the undead from focusing on any of us.

"Run!" Rafe orders, sweat pouring down his face.

No one argues. The undead army, having lost track of us, turns their attention to the only other living thing, the admin. The newcomers pours into the first railcar. Efram and Rafe move backwards, covering our retreat and I wait on the steps for them. Nathaniel is still out front, battling with the admin who hasn't yet realized he's lost control of his army.

Not long after, the hordes of undead swarm around the fat man, erasing him from sight. Nathaniel takes the opportunity to run back to the group and Efram and Rafe fall in with him.

"What about the rest of the people in the bunker?" I ask.

"You can't save them all," Nathaniel says.

"I can try," I argue.

"It's a noble goal, but one for the future, after those who must be saved are safe," the angel counters.

My stomach sinks. There has to be a way I can save them all. The admin is fighting with the undead now, and more creatures pour out of the tunnels. Their army is swelling. The locusts are regaining their senses and reforming into a swarm. If we stay here we're dead.

"Dammit," I curse, feeling helpless.

"Aviella, we do what we must," Efram says.

"We can't win them all," Rafe says, unusually serious.

I shake my head, wanting with every fiber of my being to argue with him. I want to prove them wrong. I should be able to save all these people. But I'm not an idiot. We're beyond outnumbered, and out powered. Tears well in my eyes as I come to the realization that I've done all I can. I cling to one last bit of hope that ignites like a spark inside struggling to make a fire.

"The slaves," I say, meeting each of their gazes, one at a time.

"What are you talking about?" Efram asks.

"I can't save the bunker, but I can save them," I say,

pointing at the slaves who power the railcar. "No one should be forced to work like a dog. I want to give them a choice."

"We don't have time for this," Rafe says.

"We don't have time not to do this," I counter. "We have to be better than that which we fight."

The three men exchange a look and I can tell they want to argue but almost as one they look over their shoulders at the growing army behind us.

"I can't argue with that," Rafe shrugs. "We don't have much longer."

"Fine" Nathaniel says.

Nathaniel and Rafe rush to the flat bed car that powers the train. The slaves stir to life as they climb aboard, sullenly moving to the hand pump. Rafe and Nathaniel block them by taking up positions themselves on either side of the mechanism. Grabbing hold of it, they set to work, pouring inhuman amounts of effort into powering the train.

Electricity buzzes as the batteries on the train charge, filling the air with a hum. I climb into the rail car and Efram comes with me. There's a small booth for the conductor with the control panels to my right. Efram steps into it, looks it over like he knows what he's doing, then throws several levers and pulls back on something. The train car lurches and starts to move.

A wave of weakness passes over me. It makes my knees shake and I almost collapse. Grabbing onto a pole, I hold myself up until it passes then make my way to a seat. As the train car pulls away from the station, the platform is filled with undead and buzzing locusts.

It won't be long before bunker E247 falls and I did nothing to save it.

~

I wake to the gentle swaying of the railcar. I slept deeply, peacefully, without any dreams that I can recall. Yawning and stretching, I realize that I'm lying on Efram's lap. I sit up and he smiles, his eyes soft and warm.

"Morning sleepyhead," the necroseer says.

"Morning," I say, trying to push away the last dredges of sleep.

My head is pounding, and I feel completely drained. Something about my power pulls on my body reserves when I use it. This happened the last time too, when I repelled the locusts. Eventually I need to figure this out and get a better handle on it. It would be incredibly bad to feel like this when I'm most needed.

"Is there anything to eat or drink?" I ask.

Efram chuckles playfully. I like seeing him in good spirits. His energy feels lighter, better. Like a big weight has lifted off him.

"You know these things are fully loaded, right? How do you think the admin retrieves prostitutes for the bunker's escort service?"

I frown, disgust rising at the thought. Services like that are a known factor among life in the bunkers but it's still abhorrent.

"I'm sure every surface in here isn't covered in bodily fluids, you can relax," Efram says.

I make a face but then my stomach grumbles loudly, reminding me it's been hours since I ate.

"Yeah, time to take care of that complaining stomach," Efram says.

He rises and puts his hand out to help me up. Although I don't really need it, I accept. As soon as we touch, his energy engulfs me. It's warm sunlight on my skin and makes me feel refreshed and renewed. I drink it in and realize that he's holding back his own magnetism. We smile at each other and

I see the light in his eyes but there's something more. I probe forward, trying to see past his defenses, but he puts on the brakes, pulling his hand from mine and turning away.

"There's food back here," he says.

I watch his receding back while chewing on my lower lip. I almost had it figured out. There's something about him, some reason we are the same. The train car lurches, pulling my attention to the front. Rafe and Nathaniel are working the railcar that powers this entire contraption. The slaves sit around the edges of the train watching them work. They seem to be in a state of shock. I guess it's better than being worked to death.

Rafe and Nathaniel have both taken off their shirts. Rafe has his back to me but I can watch the ripple of his muscles as he works the pump. Nathaniel I have a full on view of and my center warms in response. He is one ripped dude. His biceps move up and down and sweat covers his body in a glistening sheen. What would it be like touch him?

"Are you coming?" Efram asks, interrupting my thoughts.

My cheeks burn hot and I swallow, trying desperately to get myself under control before I turn around and my face betrays exactly what I was thinking.

"Yeah," I choke out.

Taking one deep breath and then another, heat recedes from my cheeks and only then do I turn around and follow Efram.

He leads the way to the back of the railcar in which we are currently alone. He opens the door and a strange scent comes through. It takes me a second to realize it's the smell of fresh air. A real rarity in the tunnels of the bunkers.

"Nice, isn't it?" Efram asks, smiling.

"Wow."

I haven't been above ground since I entered Protective Services when I was nine years old.

145

We enter the next car which is set up as a kitchenette. It's well stocked with plenty of supplies as well as all the necessary cooking utensils.

"Where is everyone else?" I ask.

"They're a bunch of sleeping bums in the back."

"Ah," I say, nodding my head.

Efram and I set about creating a breakfast, not just for ourselves, but for the number of people that we have with us. I make sure that we make extra because the slaves look like they're very thin and will need it. There's nothing fresh among the stores on the car but there's plenty of premade foods, oatmeal, and Nutrimeal products to make a very nice breakfast. There's even some synthetic coffee, the smell of which makes my mouth water.

The kitchenette is small so as we work Efram and I are constantly bumping into each other. Each time we touch, our energies pull to each other like a magnet. It becomes clear that Efram is a master of evasion. Every time it starts to happen, he's the one who pulls back, but each time we touch I feel a little more aware of what's going on with him. I sense his caring, his devotion.

That's such a weird thought. He barely knows me. How can he be dedicated to me? On the other hand, how can I feel about him like I do?

It's obvious that he's afraid to open his heart. I reach for a pot to make more oatmeal and my hand brushes against his. Our energies twine together and I'm sucked inside his thoughts. What I find is a huge, aching loss.

I gasp, eyes going wide. "Oh, Efram," I exhale.

He jerks his hand away from mine and says nothing. It's clear it's not something he wants to talk about and while I don't know the details I empathize. That big, empty ache inside of him is just like the hole where my father should be.

We may not talk about it, but it definitely makes me understand why I feel such a kinship to him. We've both suffered.

"Did I tell you there are books on board too?" he asks, clearly changing the subject.

I smile and my heart swells in my chest. The fact that he remembers I love vintage books is very touching.

"Where?"

"Let's finish breakfast for everyone and then I'll show you," he says.

"Okay."

Sooner or later we will go over the losses but now is not the time.

# CHAPTER SIXTEEN

*B*y the time Efram and I finish breakfast the rest of our ragtag crew is waking up. Nathaniel and Rafe climb through the conductor's area, both of their hard bodies covered in glistening sweat. Attraction swells between my thighs and I try to look anywhere but them.

"I get the shower first," Rafe says.

Nathaniel grunts, apparently unwilling to argue with the demon. Rafe laughs and pushes past me on his way to the shower. As our bodies meet, he slows. There isn't a lot of space in the rail car and he presses himself against me. If I didn't know better, I would swear he did it on purpose. He didn't, did he? My body certainly reacts like he did.

Behind the kitchenette is a dining area where everyone has gathered around a table. As we lay the food out in front of them, there's more than one grumbling belly.

"How can there be so much food?" Kress asks.

"This train was designed to go between bunkers. They had to keep it well-stocked," Efram answers.

All of them shake their heads in disbelief. I understand.

This quality of food and this much of it is unheard of in the bunkers.

"What about the former slaves?" I ask, looking at Efram.

"They refuse to leave their car," Nathaniel replies. "I will take food out to them."

I smile, feeling his warmth. He tries to suppress it but there's kindness inside of him beyond the hard exterior he faces the world with.

All of us sit at the table and eat our breakfast. Conversation is stilted. We don't really know each other, having been thrown together by the whims of fate. Things are happening fast, so much change it's hard to comprehend. It's also hard to be cheerful knowing what we left behind. That I couldn't save them.

"Look what I found!" Rafe exclaims, reemerging from the back car where the shower is.

He has two bottles, one in each hand, that he holds up triumphantly.

"Is that wine?" Zend asks.

Zed is the oldest of the group Nathaniel brought, probably in his twenties. He's dark haired and unshaven, giving him a grizzled look.

"Well, I thought this party could use a little livening up," Rafe says.

"Should we be a little more conservative with that?" Marco asks.

"Why? If we run out, Aviella can just turn more water into wine," he says with the most devilish grin I've ever seen.

A round of laughter meets his exclamation but their eyes turn to me. My cheeks burn and I wish he hadn't called attention to my mistake. Thinking about it makes my stomach queasy. Everything that has gone and the death of every single person who lived in bunker E247 is my fault. That bunker fell because of me.

Efram clears his throat, breaking the uncomfortable silence that has fallen over the train car. He glares at Rafe and the demon has the decency to look abashed.

"Okay, yeah, who can find some glasses?" Rafe asks, motioning around with the wine bottles in his hands.

One of the six rises and digs through the cabinets. This one I believe is named Kress. He looks like he's in his early twenties but his face is haggard and so drawn that he could be much older. Like all of the six, he has a haunted look to his eyes. He's seen too much, or maybe even done too much. When he finds glasses, he turns around holding them up with a smile.

"Let's start this party," Zed says.

"Now that's what I'm talking about," Rafe says.

Wine seems to help. The conversation around the table warms up and barriers start to fall. At some point or another I guess we all realize we're in this together. There's no way out except through.

Nathaniel keeps himself separated from the rest of the group, leaning against the wall with his arms crossed over his chest and scowling. It doesn't seem to matter because even his glum mood can't put a damper on the party.

Nathaniel meets my eyes and it looks like he wants to say something. Every time I look at him though I remember that canteen. I know he knows more than he's telling me about my father. One way or another I have to find out. For an instant, I almost decide not to ask at any point. If it's bad news do I want to know?

Yes, yes I do. I have to know what happened to my dad. Good or bad.

Some part of me knows it can't be bad, I would've felt it. Felt something change if he was gone. I just know it.

I take another glass of wine and sip this one slowly. A light buzz hums through my blood and my head feels light.

If I move a little too quickly, the room spins. Rafe makes sure the wine keeps flowing and even Efram begins to partake. I'm on my third glass when a girl named Anita speaks up.

"I dreamed about another trumpet," she says.

She looks at each of us at the table with sharp green eyes, flashes a worried smile, then stares at the glass in front of her.

A heavy silence falls across the table as the rest of us exchange a look. The silence starts to stretch, no one apparently willing to break it.

"It's coming soon," Anita adds.

Marco, a grim faced young man, grimaces.

"Did you have a dream too?" I ask.

"I try not to dream," he says.

"I can understand that," I offer, deciding it's best not to press. I do understand, almost all my recent dreams have been unpleasant. It makes sleep a lot less desirable.

Nathaniel stares at the floor, not looking up or joining in the conversation. As an angel I suspect he knows something about it but maybe he's sworn to silence.

"Wonderful. More beasties to play with," Rafe chimes in playfully.

Zed gulps down his wine. "They're traveling in packs and swarms."

"How do you know?" I ask.

"I've seen them. Sometimes, I see where they are, exactly," he answers.

"These gifts can be afflictions," Graham says, shaking his head.

Zed doesn't respond.

"There's a reason for them," the teenaged Junie offers.

"Every last thing that has happened has been planned, we are all part of it," Kress says.

Rafe has a fidgety look as he rises from the table. "This party need some livening up," he says.

We all look at him, waiting to see what the demon is going to do next. His grin goes from ear to ear as he drinks in our attention.

"Fictional person, three words, who am I?" he asks.

Rafe wobbles around the train car, sloshing his wine glass and slurring his words.

"The problem is not the problem, the problem is your attitude about the problem," Rafe says, waggling a finger in front of Zed's face.

He resumes stumbling around the room when suddenly it occurs to me who he's imitating.

"Captain Jack!" I exclaim.

"Very well done," Rafe says. "Of course, that means, you're up."

The demon grins from ear to ear as butterflies erupt in my stomach. I'm up? I have no idea what to do, I'm not even sure the rules of the game.

"Now now," Rafe says, taking my hands in his. "This is no time to be shy. You've got this."

He pulls me to my feet and drags me to the head of the table. Everyone's eyes are on me and my cheeks burn hot. Swallowing, I try to think of something to do. As I wrack my brain, I catch Nathaniel staring at me out of the corner of my eye. Something about seeing him triggers more memories of my dad. When I was young, before everything in the world went completely to hell, he had had a deep love of science fiction movies. That's when it comes to me.

"Once you start down the dark path, forever will it dominate your destiny, consume you it will," I say, doing my best to sound like the old Jedi that I'm trying to imitate.

Everyone at the table looks at each other, suddenly serious. Maybe not the best quote to use when we're trying to lighten the mood. My stomach tightens, and my cheeks burn even hotter. Feeling a little desperate, I try another quote.

"Do or do not. There is no try," I say, looking around the room and hoping for someone, anyone, to save me.

"Master Yoda!" Graham exclaims. "Man you had me on that first quote, I couldn't place it but I knew the voice. I was thinking maybe I had it wrong."

Everyone laughs and the tension is gone.

"Okay Graham, you're up," Rafe says.

Graham rises to his feet and moves to a position at the head of the table. He fidgets, shoving his hands in his pockets as he shifts his weight from foot to foot. He clears his throat a couple of times, shakes his head, and then looks up and meets our eyes. He pulls something out of his pocket and raises it up before his face. I stare for a long moment before it strikes me what it is.

"Is that a..." Junie gasps.

Graham pokes at the front of it, frowning, and then the sweet sound of music emerges from the device. I don't recognize the opening notes but as he plays we all look at each other. Everyone is starting to smile. Graham sways from side to side and then he burst into song.

"People are strange, when you're a stranger," Graham sings along with the song on the phone.

His voice is pretty good too. All of us laugh on cue. It doesn't take long before Kress jumps up and joins Graham, singing along to the song, followed by Marco. And just like that the apocalypse is set aside in favor of karaoke.

Rafe leans against the wall watching, a satisfied grin on his face. Even Nathaniel is swaying to the music although he doesn't sing along. People are tapping their toes, slapping out the beat on the table, or humming along. One song leads to another and everyone is taking turns flipping through the playlist on Graham's phone.

I'm grateful for it. It lightens the mood and pushes aside the fact that another trumpet is likely to sound soon. A trumpet is no laughing matter but as it is, it's a miracle we're alive at all. There will be time to figure the rest out soon enough.

I imagine life before the reckonings must've been more peaceful. No beasties to hide from, outrun, or fight. Just day-to-day living, simplicity, love, babies. The world we've inherited has none of that and it doesn't seem like any of it will ever be possible again. It's hard to maintain hope when everything seems so dark.

Rafe slips out the door and back into the other car where he found the wine. On a whim I follow. As I close the door behind me and step into the next, I sense him scan me. His power caresses across my skin like the light touch of a lover.

When I approach, he spins and grabs me by the waist, his strong hands grip tight as he presses me against the wall of the kitchenette. His eyes drink me in.

"You can get yourself in trouble throwing that sort of vibe around," he warns.

"Can't help it."

What did I just say?

The words are out but before I can take them back, his lips are on mine. The lush flick of his tongue claims my mouth unapologetically. It's like he's been waiting for this for weeks. His hands wander down my sides, over my ass, and the burning need in my core tightens until I'm going to explode.

His body presses up against mine and I feel him, big and powerful. The tension between us has been building the entire time we've known each other and now it's ready to erupt. Moaning into his kiss I open myself up, ready, but he steps back.

"Not yet," he says, shaking his head. "Not like this."

I'm panting, desperately trying to catch my breath and reign in my emotions at the same time. I stare, mouth agape. His desire pounds against me like the waves of an ocean. In a display of control that is almost unbelievable he smiles, bows, then turns and walks back into the other car.

THE TRAIN SLOWS, CAUSING EFRAM, NATHANIEL, AND RAFE TO exchange a look.

"Rock paper scissors?" Rafe asks.

"Sounds good to me," Efram answers.

Nathaniel shrugs and steps up to the other two men. They perform rock paper scissors and Nathaniel was immediately knocked out. Rafe and Efram playoff against each other and Rafe loses.

"Damn it," Rafe says, shaking his head. "Well, back to the grindstone."

Rafe and Nathaniel move through the conductor's booth and then out onto the front car that powers the train. I watch as they take up positions on either side of the pump and set to work recharging the batteries. The former slaves watch them with a look of awe on their face. It seems they still can't believe that it's no longer their job.

Watching the men work I see a light up ahead. It stirs distant memories.

"Is that?" I ask, pointing ahead.

Efram come to stand beside me. His energy is warm, comfortable, and comforting all at the same time.

"Yeah," he says. "I told you these cars are designed for going outside. We're about to emerge."

Everyone gathers towards the front. We've been underground so long I haven't seen the sun in almost a decade. I wonder if it still looks the same. I also wonder what horrors await us.

The train car rattles and jerks and most of us lose our footing. Efram catches me and keeps me from falling.

"Careful there," he says, holding me firmly in his hands.

The sky is a dusky blue much as I remember. The sun is too far overhead to see from inside the car. The land around us is a wasteland. It looks like a bomb went off and maybe it did. The governments launched everything they had when the wars broke out. Not all of the devastation was caused by angels and demons.

Blasted land stretches out for as far as the eye can see. Broken pieces of trees reach for the sky breaking up the landscape. Rubble lies in piles that once might have been homes or businesses. Fortunately, nothing else greets us.

I take a seat and watch the landscape rolling past. Somewhere out there is my dad. Or maybe he's in one of the other bunkers. One way or another I'm going to find him. I know, deep in my bones, that he's alive.

"So where are we heading?" I ask.

"Nathaniel says we should make for Bunker 2," Efram answers.

"Isn't that one of the mega bunkers?" Anita asks.

"Yeah," Efram says.

"I've heard those are even worse than the smaller bunkers like E247," Anita responds.

"It depends," Efram says. "I'm sure we'll be fine."

The conversation is interrupted by Junie screaming. It cuts through the air and sets my nerves on edge. Everyone whips around, looking for the source of danger. Something, I don't know what, pounds against my awareness. It's making it hard to breathe.

"What is it?" I ask.

"Behind us!" Marco answers.

The entire train rattles. Dishes fall out of the cabinets and things sitting on the table rattle to the floor. The sound of breaking glass and shouting people fills the air.

Trying to steady myself, I make my way to the back of the car. When I look out the rear window my mouth goes dry and my stomach drops. I don't know what the hell that thing is but it's huge. The monster is a crazy crossbreed of multiple animals thrown together in some horrific nightmare.

It's almost twelve feet tall and must be eight feet wide. It has four human arms, the head of a crocodile, and the body of a man. Its jaw snaps open and shut as it chases the train. It slams its body against the rear car, causing everything to vibrate again. I'm tossed off my feet and land on my butt.

"Oh no," Zed cries out. "What we do about that?"

The buzz returns, building inside of me. I'm not sure what I can do against this thing, but I have to try.

"Aviella, don't," Efram yells.

I whip my head around and look at him, ready to argue. He races across the car and leaps into the conductor's booth. He throws switches wildly and then the train jerks into faster motion.

The thing chasing us howls, a bone chilling sound that doesn't fit the size of the monstrosity. It continues chasing us, but the train is pulling away.

"That thing must have escaped from Wormwood," Graham says.

"Are you serious?" I ask.

"The government was doing all kinds of messed up things in there, and we're not that far away," Graham responds.

We huddle around the rear windows and watch until the thing disappears from sight. The image of that monstrosity will be burned in my mind forever. Whatever the military was doing in Wormwood, it's given birth to some of the ugliest, most disturbing looking beasts I've ever seen.

Only once it's completely out of sight do we breathe a collective sigh of relief. We take up positions around the car and silently contemplate what's next.

The land outside the car changes. It looks less like a bomb went off and more like an area of long neglect. There's grass growth and other weeds making things green. A few buildings are still standing. The train car slows.

"What are we doing?" I ask.

"We're out of fuel," Efram answers. "I had to pull down the entire battery to get away from that thing. We need to stop for a little bit and recharge."

"Is that Bunker 4?" Graham asks.

"We shouldn't stop here," Nathaniel says, stepping into the conductor booth.

"We don't have the power to carry on," Efram replies. "We need to charge the battery. Besides, there could be supplies here."

"We must not go into Bunker 4," Nathaniel intones.

"Why not?" Rafe asks.

"We can't, we must not," Nathaniel says and there's an air of desperation to his words. "We have to steer clear of it."

He knows something that he's not telling us. I guess I shouldn't be surprised, it is Nathaniel after all.

"Restocking our supplies isn't a bad idea," Efram says.

"It'd be nice to get out and stretch our legs," I say.

"Uh, guys?" Kress asks.

"I'm telling you we should not go in there, it is a very bad idea," Nathaniel says.

"Yeah but you're a scaredy-cat," Rafe answers, unable to give up a chance of poking fun at the angel.

Nathaniel glares, crossing his arms over his chest. Rafe just grins.

"Nathaniel if you can't give me a better reason than just you say so then we're going to go in there," Efram says.

"Guys!" Kress exclaims.

"What!" Efram yells.

"We have to move, now!" Kress responds.

Everyone turns and looks. He's pale and pointing out the back window. Pounding up the rail line is the monster that we just out ran. Every time one of his massive legs hits the ground clouds of dust puff up and now that I'm paying attention it feels like the ground vibrates as well.

"Oh God," I gasp.

"That's our signal," Rafe says, leaping through the conductor booth and out onto the front platform car.

Nathaniel joins him as does Efram. A moment later Graham and Zed are there as well. They grab onto the handles of the pump and work furiously to charge the battery.

"Aviella," Efram yells. "Pull that lever to the right, throw the switches on the left."

Stepping into the conductor booth I stare at the foreign controls. I have no idea what I'm doing but I try to follow his directions. Slowly, so slow it's painful, the train starts to move. Looking over my shoulder, the monster is closing with us.

"Guys, we need more," I yell.

Somehow, they pump harder. The buzz of electricity flowing towards the battery grows and the train jerks, moving a little bit faster. Looking ahead the horizon dips away. It takes me a minute to figure it out but were coming up on a hill. As the power car goes over the top the train picks up momentum and then we're moving even faster, gravity pulling us down.

Everyone cheers as the monstrosity is left behind. Hopefully it will give up chasing us. I guess the decision to avoid Bunker 4 was taken out of our hands. I wonder if that's not fate too.

The former slaves volunteer to work the pump for a while, giving the rest a break. They climb back into the car and sit around looking exhausted. The air between all of us is heavy.

"Well, maybe things will be better when we reach Bunker 2," Marco says.

"The mega bunkers are not any better than the smaller settlements," Nathaniel says.

"What do you mean?" Anita asks.

"There is even less privacy and in general the controls aren't as easy to get around. You should prepare yourselves," Nathaniel answers.

"Great, I didn't think it could get any worse than where we were," Zed says.

"Steer clear of the notion we're headed to the promised land. We're not," Nathaniel says.

"We're survivors, wherever we wind up," Efram chimes in.

Efram doesn't seem fazed either way and I agree with him. I'm sure we'll have to face trouble in any direction we take. Nathaniel's desperation to avoid Bunker 4 bothers me, in a nagging sort of way. Once again, I feel like he's keeping something secret that I deserve to know. The angel is good at that, witness his refusal to tell me anymore about my dad. Pursing my lips, I decide right then I'm going to find out the truth, no matter what it takes.

# CHAPTER SEVENTEEN

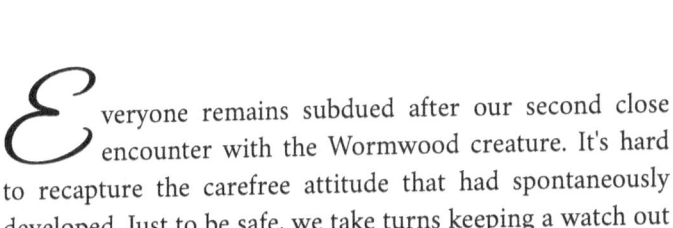

*E*veryone remains subdued after our second close encounter with the Wormwood creature. It's hard to recapture the carefree attitude that had spontaneously developed. Just to be safe, we take turns keeping a watch out the back window. It's better than being taken by surprise again.

Nathaniel, Efram, and Rafe take turns at the pump with the former slaves lending their aid as well. The next several hours pass uneventful and quiet. Conversation is returned to being stilted and uncomfortable. I wonder if everyone else has had a similar life to mine. No one here seems to have social skills, which goes hand-in-hand with the territory of being an outcast.

Rowan sits next to me holding my hand. I love the flow of her energy, so calm and upbeat. There are so many things I want to say to her, but I don't know the words. It's all spinning emotions and feelings that I don't know how to express.

"I don't want to lose you," I whisper.

The sadness in her eyes is all the answer I need. She shakes her head side-to-side and cups my cheek with her hand. Suddenly she smiles and pulls me against her and I know that no matter what she'll always be my friend.

The train slows, breaking the moment. Rising to my feet I go to the conductor booth and look out. There's a flashing red light ahead of us, which is unusual enough, but it also looks like something is wrong with the tracks. The hairs on the back of my neck stand up and a tingle runs through my nervous system. This has all the makings of a trap.

"Damn it," Efram curses.

"What is it?" I ask.

"Nothing good," he says.

Nathaniel pushes past us and pulls a couple of levers then throws some switches causing the train car to come to a stop. Rafe emerges from the back and makes his way up to the rest of us. Once the train is at a stop the three men quietly disembark.

I watch them approach the blinking red lights, sensing their alertness. Each of them is scanning the area with their power as well as looking with their eyes. Their individual powers pass over my skin. Each of them is so unique I can tell the differences just by their energy.

Nathaniel crouches down on the tracks inspecting something. Efram and Rafe stand guard. I watch without breathing, my heart pounding in my chest, knowing in any moment something is going to happen.

"What is it?" Marco asks, suddenly behind me.

I jump involuntarily, spinning to face him. "Don't do that!"

He throws his hands up in front of himself and takes a step back. "Hey, sorry!"

My power surges within my blood and it takes me a moment to get it under control. Swallowing hard and shaking my head I wait until the surge recedes.

"It's fine," I say. "My nerves are on edge."

Behind Marco the rest of the six stare, scared and waiting to be told what's happening.

"There's something wrong with the tracks, I don't know what's happening," I tell them. "The guys are looking into it."

I'm trying to fend off an increasing feeling of dread but can't shake it. Something bad is coming, closer and closer, I feel it approaching.

"Dead things, I feel them," Junie says, her voice quavering.

"Where?" I ask, at the same time a loud thud hits side of the railcar.

The car rocks side to side throwing all of us off balance. I slam into the wall hard enough to leave a bruise, cursing.

The land outside the railcar explodes. Dead things leap out of the dirt all around us. Junie lets out a scream and I resist the urge to do the same. It looks like they're everywhere, we're surrounded.

The door at the front bursts open and Nathaniel leaps through, his eyes glowing pale white. He rushes in front of me and takes up a defensive stance.

"Prepare for battle," he orders.

"I can help --" I start to say but something hits me.

It's not physical at all, but it takes my energy. I'm drained, my power being sucked out of me. I reach for my gifts, the familiar buzz, but I can't find it. It's like it's gone.

My head spins and I'm gasping air. It's all I can do to stay standing. The room rocks back and forth and my vision is gray at the edges. It's like everyone is way far away down a long tunnel.

Rowan rushes over to stand next to me and takes my hand. She mimes something, but I can't figure out what she's trying to tell me. I shake my head in response.

The six form arc in front of Nathaniel. The dead things are pounding on the car and glass breaks. They're climbing through the broken windows. It won't be long before we're overwhelmed. I have to help.

Once more I reach but my power isn't there. It feels like my gifts are being sucked away.

Nathaniel's eyes glow with protective fury as he speaks in an ancient, angelic tongue. I know what he means. He's commanding the dead things to stay away. Outside Rafe and Efram are slicing through the creatures, fighting their way into the train.

There must be a source, something is draining me. I don't know what it is, but I have to stop it. My knees buckle and in desperation I grab Nathaniel by his shoulders, holding myself up.

The dead are swarming in, overwhelming. There's too many. We can't hold out. Desperate I look for any way out. The door to the rear of the train car bursts open. I look with a momentary glimmer of hope expecting Rafe or Efram coming to our rescue but my heart sinks. A dark figure looms in the door, flowing black rags obscure its form. A giant hood covers its face, casting it in shadow out of which glow two red eyes like hot coals.

"Who the hell let Harry Potter in here?" Marco quips, turning and blasting the figure with a burst of his power.

The thing waves its hand, languidly, pushing aside Marco's power like it's no more than an annoying mosquito.

That thing is the source of the problem. It raises an arm, pointing a skeletal finger at me. My energy is pulled out, that thing is siphoning it. Groaning, I fall to my knees. The undead press up against the six and they try to hold against them using their powers the best they can. Nathaniel curses as he continues commanding them back. There's too many.

"Crap," Graham swears, leaping over a body to land between me and that thing.

Graham raises his hands, fingers weaving as he focuses

his power. The thing, whatever it is, doesn't seem to notice him. Kress moves to stand beside Graham. Their powers glow around them with the golden-green energy they are weaving together. They're trying to bind the thing. Strands of power snake out from their hands, encircling it.

Sweat is pouring down Graham's brow and he's panting. The strands circle the thing then jerk tight, forcing it to drop its arm. The drain on me stops, leaving me empty and burned out. The thing turns its hooded head, focusing on the two in front of it. It shakes its head then there's a low rumbling sound that grows louder, vibrating the floor.

Darkness explodes out of the thing like a dark sun bursting into life. It's blinding my aura sight. Gasping, I blink rapidly, trying to process if I'm really blind. Exhaustion lies so heavy on me that I can barely move. Rubbing my eyes, my vision clears and I see the room around me but I can't see auras.

Rowan kneels beside me, her mouth open and shaking her head side-to-side. Her eyes glow and something in her changes. She kisses my forehead then rises and turns on a heel. She raises her arms, holding them out above her head. All the deadies stop and look up like there's something over their heads. I can barely keep myself awake I'm so tired, but I have to. I need to know what's happening.

The undead tremble as Rowan waves her arms in the air and then closes her fists. The undead around us fall to the ground, actually dead.

Rowan collapses to the floor.

"Rowan!" I scream.

Whatever Rowan did also affected the shrouded thing. It's not dead dead like the others but it is blasted backwards through the door. I reach for my power, trying to draw on it for strength. It's still suppressed, like there's a wall between me and it.

I look at the thing and see a hazy line between it and I. It looks like it's still siphoning off my energy. I open my mouth to scream but I can't find the strength. It's all I can do to hold myself up on my arms.

Everything fades, blackness reaches for me. My heart slows, pounding thuds in my chest. It's hard to breathe. I'm fading fast.

Digging as deep as I can, I crawl over to Rowan, desperate, she has to be okay. When I reach her I can't tell if she's breathing. I'm too tired to hold my head up so I lie down on her chest. She has to be okay.

Nathaniel leaps over me. When he lands, the train car feels like it jumps, making me bounce up off the floor and back down, banging my chin. He glows with a golden white light so bright I shield my eyes. There's a flutter and his wings burst out as he reveals himself and his full angelic glory. He shouts something in a tongue I don't understand. Power bursts out of him like a nuclear blast.

The thing, whatever it is, screams a high-pitched eardrum tearing sound that rips through my body. The block on my power is gone but I'm left exhausted. My body is heavy, too heavy to work with.

Pulling my head off Rowan's chest I place my hands on her face. A tear lands on her and trails its way across her cheek.

"Rowan," I whisper.

## CHAPTER EIGHTEEN

*N*athaniel scoops me into his arms. He's warm against my skin, like a toaster oven. I try to put my arms around his neck to help alleviate my weight, but they won't respond. It's all I can do to keep my head from lolling around like my neck is broken.

"Rowan," I say, it comes out as a whisper.

"Rafe!" Nathaniel barks.

"I got it," I hear Rafe say.

Nathaniel carries me through the train car, carefully turning sideways to avoid bumping my head as he moves between the cars and back to the bunks. I've never felt so exhausted in all of my life. I have nothing left. It goes beyond muscle tired, it's a deep-down bone weariness. All my reserves are gone.

Nathaniel kneels next to one of the bunks and holds me with one arm, keeping me close against his chest. He pulls down the blanket before laying me down and then covers me over.

I'm emotional, I want to cry, but even that is too much effort. The angel, his stunning eyes so close to mine, leans in and places a hand on my cheek. The concern in his eyes is mirrored in the energy between us. The barriers he keeps up between the two of us soften like he wants to let them down. I wish he would, I want him to let me in.

I open my mouth intending to say something, I'm not sure what, anything, but no sound comes out. Nathaniel smiles, nods, then rises to his feet and steps aside. Rafe carries Rowan in and she doesn't appear to be awake. My heart leaps into my throat and my stomach sinks. Surely they wouldn't be carrying her back here if she was...

"Is she?" I croak.

"She will recover," Nathaniel reassures me.

Relief floods through me and I pass out.

～

"You need to eat," Efram says.

His voice pulls me out of a very deep sleep. I try to open my eyes but it feels like they're crusted shut with a weeks' worth of sand. Sleep claws at me, not wanting to let me go, and I really want to just go back into it. Eating seems is entirely too much effort to bother.

Efram isn't going to have any of that. He hooks an arm behind my shoulders and then he's lifting me into a sitting position. He places my back is against the wall and I sit there still unable to open my eyes. A wet cloth touches my forehead, dabbing across it and then wipes off my eyes and at last I'm able to open them and see him sitting in front of me. I give him a smile, or my best attempt, I'm sure it probably fails miserably.

He sets the wet cloth aside and grabs a bowl moving it between the two of us. With infinite patience he feeds me a spoonful at a time. It's a plain broth but incredibly satisfying. As I take it down I feel a glimmer of strength returning.

When I have taken all I can, I have enough strength shake my head side-to-side.

"No more," I whisper. I can't seem to make my voice any louder.

"Okay," Efram says. "You did good."

He helps me to lie back down and places the cover over me. Once I'm settled he climbs up onto the top bunk and helps Rowan. I watch his feet dangling over the side of the bunk for a while before sleep claims me again.

WHEN I WAKE UP THE NEXT TIME ROWAN IS SITTING ON THE edge of my bunk. She smiles brightly when she sees my eyes open. This time I feel certain I can return the smile and do so. Rowan lies down on the bunk next to me and pulls me into a tight embrace. My arms respond, at last, and I return the hug. She bounces up off the bunk onto her feet, dancing around the room ecstatically. It warms my heart seeing her feel so good and happy. She stops and taps a finger on her chin looking thoughtful.

She holds one hand in front of her face with a closed fist and flourishes her other arm out and around in the air. It takes me a minute before I recognize what she's doing.

"Rafe!" I exclaim.

She grins and nods excitedly. She moves through a series of mimes which lifts my spirits as she imitates all of our companions for me to guess which one she's pretending to be. It helps pass the time. I sense the car is moving but I have no idea how far we are from our destination.

After a while, the door to the car opens, letting in the clatter of the steel train wheels rolling along the track and the slight whoosh of wind. The door slides closed and Efram steps up beside Rowan.

"You should go eat," he says, motioning with the bowl in his hands and back towards the door.

Rowan nods then comes over to the bunk and sits on the edge. Leaning in, she gives me a big hug and a kiss on the cheek. She stares into my eyes until I nod, letting her know that it's okay for her to go. We grip hands and our fingers linger on each other as she pulls away and then she's gone.

Efram helps me back into a sitting position and feeds me again. Apparently having your energy sucked out of you is incredibly draining. It's still almost more effort than I can manage to lift my arms.

"This sucks," I say.

"I'm amazed you survived at all," Efram remarks. "We almost lost you."

There's more behind his words then just the grimness of the statement. I'm certain he would be devastated if anything happened to me.

"You ought to know by now you can't get rid of me that easily," I quip, echoing his own words back to him.

He smiles and shakes his head. I finish the soup and while I'm feeling better, I'm still nowhere near back to hundred percent. The exhaustion comes fast.

"I'd like to lay down again," I say.

"Of course," he says.

I realize as he helps me that it's dark outside. Maybe it's not so bad that I'm sleepy. Once he helps me position myself back in the bed he climbs under the covers with me and wraps his body around me. His energy engulfs me the same as his body does and his heart beats a steady rhythm against my back. I feel something that it seems like I haven't felt in forever. Safe. It isn't long before I'm asleep again.

～

WHEN I WAKE UP I'M ALONE, WHICH IS ANOTHER THING I can't recall the last time happened. Life in the bunkers doesn't allow for time to be alone and I find myself relishing the moment.

Even in the showers, at least among the lower classes, you don't get any time to process your day or think about it. Under the meager water spray, you have five minutes or less. Wash up, dress, start your day. Dimly I remember a time when living was possible. When there were more than just snatched bits of time in a sequence of hope squashing events.

Sure, even before the apocalypse my dad kept us on the move. Sometimes we'd live in the mountains out of a tent. Other times we would have apartments in the cities. We were never in one place for very long, but it didn't matter because we had each other. Damn, I miss him so much.

What is all this for? Why isn't it just over? Why are we still alive?

It's a momentary fit that I wouldn't call despair or depression but it's probably edging towards that. So much has happened and everything keeps getting worse.

The door to the car slides open and shut. I'm feeling quite a bit better and can sit up on my own now, so I do. Nathaniel pokes his head around the corner looking grim as ever.

Somehow, it's fitting that the angel shows up in one of my rare moments of hopeless thinking. The expression on his face surprises me though, maybe I look worse than I think.

"What can I say, being energy drained is rough on the body," I quip, trying to make light of the situation.

His grim expression doesn't change. He holds up a pudding cup and my eyes go wide.

"Seriously!" I exclaim excitedly.

"If you don't want it," he says, lowering the cup to his side.

"Oh no you don't," I yelp, leaping to my feet and grabbing it from his hand.

My head spins with the effort but I manage to plop myself back down on the bed before anything more catastrophic happens. Cracking it open my mouth is already watering. The sweet smell of butterscotch drifts to my nostrils. I inhale deeply and hold, savoring it before I ever take a bite. When I open my eyes, Nathaniel is holding out a spoon which I gratefully take. Slipping the first spoonful into my mouth is like putting a piece of heaven on my tongue.

"You like it?" Nathaniel asks, his voice still sonorous.

"Oh my God," I say, and put another spoonful in my mouth.

Nathaniel pulls a small stool over and sits down, watching me eat the pudding cup.

"They're targeting you," he announces finally.

"The dead things?" I ask.

He stares at me with his striking and unreadable eyes. He shakes his head and looks away. Well clearly it's something worse than the dead things. Great!

"Their shadow masters," he says. "There's something special and you're... special above special. They want to take you apart, inside and out if they can."

"I'd like to vote against that option," I say, trying to bring some levity to the situation.

He stares into my eyes and it feels like he sees me, past all the front I put on, past the social niceties straight to me.

"For a second there..." he says, trailing off.

His concern is clear in his expression but more than that I feel the walls he keeps up between the two of us relaxing. I'm getting a sense of him behind them.

"I'm fine," I say, trying to be reassuring.

"We have to get you warded properly before we go anywhere. That... can't happen again," he says.

"Warded?" I ask.

"Protectively marked," he replies.

He lifts his sleeve and I see several faintly glowing tattoos decorate his arm.

"And we need to train you, in a number of things. You're part of the end time events. My blood tells me you're an integral part. I believe we're meant to prepare you and there will be more who will assist you too."

I take in the information and process it in the background because most of my thoughts are dominated by what he said. I'm special above special. What does that mean?

"What makes me so special?"

Nathaniel shakes his head, dropping his eyes from mine. "I don't know."

He's telling me the truth. Since we're having a moment of truth telling I decide to ask the one burning question I have for the angel. Maybe I can get that truth out of him also.

"What do you know about my dad?"

He meets my eyes and his jaw tightens. The tension between the two of us builds.

Before he speaks, the world tilts on its axis, causing me to gasp and grip the bunk on either side.

"What in the hell was that?" I ask, panting and looking around frantic.

## CHAPTER NINETEEN

There's a popping sound and several yelps from the other car. Instinctively, I'm on my feet and moving for the door before my body has time to respond, letting me know it's still weak. I grab the wall to steady myself and Nathaniel grips my waist, for which I'm grateful.

There's a pull in my blood, something I can't put my finger on, it doesn't feel bad necessarily but more like something is going to happen. It feels like a shoe is about to drop but I don't know what that shoe is or what it means.

I shake my head to clear it as I go through the door and cross over to the other car. When I throw open the door the four mages I met before stand at the far end in a small huddle.

Almost as one they focus on me and their energy scans me. I smile but it's obvious they're veiling much deeper concerns. Something about their unplanned and unannounced arrival raises my hackles.

"What are you guys doing here?" I ask.

"Got to love a girl who's straight to the point," Gavin replies, turning on his full charm.

His ever-present smile reaches his eyes with the same glimmer as the Cheshire cat, like he knows something I don't. Something that either he or I will be amused by when the mystery he's keeping is unveiled.

Nathaniel stands behind me protectively close but doesn't say anything. I don't see Efram or Rafe so they must be out at the pump powering the train. Rowan and the other six are seated at the table looking back and forth between me and the mages.

Killian makes his way through the tight space towards me. He stops directly in front of me and holds his hands out about a foot off of me. He pauses and tilts his head to one side.

"May I?" he asks.

"May you what?"

He smiles and his energy passes across me in waves.

"We're checking up on you," Ronan says, from behind him.

I shrug hesitantly, giving my consent. Killian places his hands on my midsection and closes his eyes. A moment later they open and lock with mine. A tingle runs through me as he does something and then it's over.

"You can't take another energy hit like that. You're strong but you need to be healed and warded. Quickly," Killian says.

"I was just telling her that same thing," Nathaniel says over my shoulder.

Luca comes up on my other side and holds his hands up, one over my midsection and one by my head. His eyes roll closed and a wave of weakness passes over me. I see some of my energy lifts off of me like a fog and then it zips to him. His eyes snap open and he looks over his shoulder at Ronan, nodding.

"She's clear," Luca says.

"It might be best if we do this next part somewhere

more... private," Gavin says, his eyes darting around the room.

"Why private?" I ask.

Gavin's grin widens and he shakes his head. It's obvious I'm not going to get a straight answer out of him.

"Fine."

The mages follow while Nathaniel remains behind with the others. Once we enter the other car, I turn and face them with my arms crossed over my chest.

"Now what is all about?"

The four men exchange a look and I know in my gut that they understand each other without words. Which makes me more annoyed with them. I lock eyes with Ronan and grit my teeth. Arching an eyebrow, I will him to answer me.

There's barely a slight buzz as my power tries to rise to my call. I'm still wiped after my ordeal and I'm nowhere near the power level I normally am.

Luca walks past me and stops when he gets behind me. Gavin moves to my left, Killian to my right, and Ronan strides up in front of me with his cocky devil may care attitude.

"We're going to heal your energy," Gavin says, his eyes alight with delight.

"I got that," I say. "It doesn't actually explain anything."

"Some things have to be experienced," Gavin says, grinning wider.

There's something in the way he looks at me or maybe it's his words but suddenly I'm shy. I can't meet his eyes, and I'm acutely aware of being surrounded by four very attractive men. I feel their presence and their energy pressing against mine just as clearly as if they were pressing up against my body. Just for an instant my imagination runs wild and my cheeks flush.

No, I'm not going there, no way.

The tightness in my core gives lie to the control I'm trying to assert. Ronan hunches down so that he's eye level with me. Slowly he raises his hands and holds them in front of my shoulders palms facing me.

"I don't feel anything," I say.

Out of the corners my eyes Killian and Gavin have raised their hands as well and I can assume that Luca has done the same at my back. All four of the mages have their hands at the same height, palms facing me and creating a box around me. I wait for something exciting to happen, but nothing comes. My patience is running thin.

"A moment," Ronan says, like he's reading my thoughts.

Maybe he is, if so that would suck. If he picked up on my thoughts about the four of them.... how about we just go with no he's not?

I focus on my breathing and listen to my heart beating slow and steady in my chest. As I focus on trying to relax, a gentle tingling sensation starts. It's strange because it feels like it's about two feet away from me. When I focus on the sensation it comes to me that I'm feeling where the mages hands are. They're the source point from which it emanates.

Suddenly my breath catches in my chest as the tingle moves into me. Passing over my skin and causing a feeling of lightness. It moves through and my insides become warm. It's like drinking wine. The four mages hum, a low, steady monotonous tone. My insides match the vibration. The tingle becomes something more, something in my bones. It's almost like the buzz used to be whenever my power would activate before I had any understanding of it.

It grows inside of me until it's a hard thumping. They move their hands closer, barely an inch away from my skin. Warmth spreads from where they are. My body responds, involuntarily, and a shudder runs down my spine. My core become so tight it's going to explode. Worse yet Ronan's eyes are locked on my breasts. His lips part and every fiber of me wants to taste them. Luca is so close to my back I feel his breath on my neck. Killian and Gavin lean in, their fingertips brushing my arms.

I tear my eyes away from Ronan, I can't look into his anymore. His desire is too clear. It doesn't do any good because when I drop my eyes his desire is even plainer to see through his pants. My mouth goes dry and my heart pounds in my chest. Energy surges through my body.

I will give myself to them. I'll take them all. I want them in ways I've never ever felt before. It seems right, natural. So much energy pours into me I'm going to explode. I'm a sparkling fountain on the fourth of July, shooting sparks into the sky. Pretty colors dancing around me. I see it in the air around us as my power and my energy blends with that of the four mages every nerve in my body is alive and hypersensitive. The air moving in the car, the slight musty smell, the dirt outside the car as we travel down the rail. My heart is beating so hard it has to stop or I'm going to have a heart attack. I can't breathe.

The four men come closer, their bodies brush against mine. Everywhere they touch a fire ignites. Something shifts and I take control. Where at first they were giving the energy to me, now I'm taking it. Drinking it in like a person dying of thirst. Replenishing my reserves, I absorb it and demand more, pulling it from them.

Ronan's eyes widen and he gasps. I drink him in, pulling more out of him, pulling from all of four of them. Their desires, their hopes, and their dreams. They have such depths of power, such reserves that I've never felt before. It's like they're bottomless wells. I want to take them. I want to ride them and make them mine.

I step back inside my own head and realize what I'm doing, draining them of their very life force. Seeing it for what it is, I stop. The four mages take a step away from me. I meet Gavin's eyes and he smiles, but it's tentative, less confident. I pointedly avoid looking at what I can clearly see out of my peripheral vision is happening in his pants. For his part he avoids looking at my chest and the parts of me that are poking through my shirt. I'm grateful for that.

The door behind Ronan opens and Nathaniel strides in. He stops and stares and his jaw tightens.

"She needs to rest now," he says, annoyance clear in his voice.

"Yeah, good idea," Gavin agrees.

My body slowly acclimates to its new condition and as it does a deep tiredness follows. I can't suppress a yawn.

"Thanks," I say, tentatively.

I'm not used to these feelings or experiencing such overwhelming desires. It feels awkward and I'm unsure how to proceed past it. Ronan nods and then leaves with the other mages in tow. Nathaniel stands a short distance away and looks over at the bunk beds.

"You should get some sleep," he says.

"Yeah, good idea."

I climb into the bed and I'm asleep before my head hits the pillow.

I WAKE UP RAVENOUS. I DON'T THINK I'VE EVER BEEN SO hungry in all my life. Nathaniel is sitting on a stool watching me. Somehow the angel manages to do this without being completely creepy.

"Good morning," I greet him, seeing the sun streaming through the windows of the train car.

"Morning," he replies. "How are you today?"

I stretch before answering. Everything aches, but I feel a million times better despite that.

"Sore," I say. "Although overall, I feel amazing."

"You're adjusting to absorbing so much energy," he says. "It will take a little time."

"Ah," I nod. "I guess that makes sense. I'm starving."

"Breakfast is ready for you," he says.

I bounce out of bed with a spring in my step and a feeling of strength I haven't felt in a really long time. Taking a deep breath, my body feels alive. My senses are enhanced somehow and I'm aware of every little thing around me. It's beautiful.

Nathaniel leads the way to the other car where the rest of the innocents greet me. Junie places down a bowl of Nutrimeal, two slices of toast, and a magically red apple. I sit and inhale the food, barely taking time to taste it.

"Once you're fed I will ward you with ceremonial symbols," Nathaniel says.

"Okay," I agree, around a mouthful of food.

*I* watch Aviella eat her breakfast. It's obvious she's been reinvigorated and I have a very good idea of how that happened. What I'm not sure is how I feel about it. The four mages manage to keep to themselves even in the cramped quarters of the train car. I know they have loose ties to Efram and Nathaniel, but I don't have any experience with them. It leaves me wondering, not only about their usefulness but their true intentions.

As far as I know the entire mage order was wiped out years ago, so how strong can they actually be? Are they really mages or are they a front for something else? Some upper level shadow powers certainly could use mages as a tool for their machinations.

Their interest in Aviella means I'm interested in them. I'm not going to blindly trust them just because Efram and Nathaniel do. That's not enough weight for me to let them slide by on. I want to know what their real interest is and I'm uniquely qualified to find out.

Aviella finishes her breakfast and then leaves the car with Nathaniel. It's good that the angel is good toward her. It's a skill uniquely his and we're going to need all the advantages we can get. I'm getting a sense of the shadow forces that are coming after her and it's scary as hell, literally.

It also gives me an opportunity to confront the mages. As I approach their apparent leader, the one they call Ronan, he turns to face me. As I square off with him he straightens, raising to his full height and a magical shield coalesces from his energy. The three with him stiffen, focusing on me too. He's trying to establish dominance. That's fine, he doesn't know what he's dealing with. I smile as the thrill of confrontation shoots through me.

"Why are you here, really?" I ask.

"Straight and to the point, unusual for a demon," Ronan responds.

"I'm way beyond your average demon."

"I can see that."

Strangely, he relaxes and the shield dissipates. The three mages behind him also loosen their stances and we all back down from the edge of confrontation.

"Now that we've gotten past all of that," I say, keeping my smile firmly in place, "how about you answer my question."

"We're all here for the same reason... mostly," Ronan replies.

"If I believed that, I wouldn't be standing here questioning you."

"She has to be protected, and she needed our help," Ronan says.

"And I, for one, am eternally grateful. Now why are you really here," I repeat.

Ronan smiles but it doesn't reach his unusually green eyes. He glances over my shoulder at the far end of the car where the six are gathered.

"Them?" I ask, unable to keep the surprise out of my voice.

"They cannot go to the bunker with you. It would change their fate in a way that would certainly endanger all," Ronan says.

"All who?"

"All who still live on this scorched planet," he responds.

I'm an expert in lies. They've been my stock in trade for millennia. No one can lie to me, I can sense it if they do. The fact that he isn't makes my stomach sink. A desire to protect the six from these mages flares inside of me, burning its way through my limbs.

"I thought your entire order was wiped out," I counter, changing tactics.

"Almost all of us," Ronan agrees, and there's a depth of sadness behind his words, reinforcing that he speaks true.

"So, what's your business with them?" I ask.

"We're meant to protect them."

"Protect who?" Efram asks, arriving just in time.

"The six," I say.

Ronan shakes his head. "No, all seven."

"Seven!" I say, eyes widening.

Gavin nods firmly.

"You can't take Rowan," Efram says before I can. "It will destroy Aviella."

"It's not up for debate. You know I'm telling the truth," Ronan says, staring at me.

"Who the hell are you guys?" Efram asks.

"They are the last remnants of the Order of Mages," I tell him. "At least they believe they are."

"That can't be, the Order was wiped out," Efram responds.

I shake my head side to side. "Apparently not."

"But they..." Efram trails off.

"Yeah," I agree.

The Order of Mages were magical Titans whose entire purpose was to go up against arch demons. They fought to preserve souls who were protectively marked as part of the Grand Scheme. They were supposed to have been destroyed decades ago. The entire Crusades were a cover-up for their destruction.

"Then that means," Efram says, staring into my eyes.

"Yeah," I nod.

"Damn."

## CHAPTER TWENTY-ONE

"**W**hat's next," I ask, turning to face Nathaniel.
"I'll need you to go into the shower," he says.

"You're kidding, right?"

I can tell by the look on his face he's not kidding. What else should I expect from the angel? I'm fairly sure there's not a funny feather in his entire body. Resigning myself to following the angel's orders, I make my way through the car to the showers. When I pull aside the first one's curtain, I find markings on the floor.

"You'll need to undress," Nathaniel says.

"No way," I say, cheeks burning like fire with self-consciousness.

I already have a hard time hiding my feelings with everything that happened with the mages and now he wants me to get naked in front of him? Yeah, how about no.

"I'm sorry, it's necessary," he says. "The sigils must be on your bare skin."

Biting my lower lip, I remind myself I decided to comply with him. Instinctively, I know he's right, in that part of me from where my power comes. I nod my agreement and start to undress. Before I undo the first button, Nathaniel turns his back like a gentleman. I'm grateful for the consideration.

"Okay," I say once I'm finished.

He holds a towel out without turning around which I gratefully take. I hook it around myself and then he turns and looks me over.

"Step into the shower, center yourself in the runes I've drawn on the floor," he orders.

Looking at the runes on the floor, I almost know what they are, it's like something that's on the tip of your tongue but you can't quite recall. I feel like I should know what they mean. Sighing, I push that aside and step in the shower, centering myself as instructed.

Nathaniel walks in with me. The showers on the train are not meant for more than one person, making him be intimately close, especially considering that I'm mostly naked. After my experience with the mages my sex drive has been out of control. I'm acutely aware of him and can only pray he isn't picking up on it.

Gently, he takes my shoulders and turns me so that I'm facing away from him. His fingers trace lines across my back and up my neck. A thrill runs through my nerves and I suppress a shiver. I like the way his hands feel, soft yet firm. Cool lines trail behind his fingertips on my skin. Enticing, inviting, it's definitely not helping with my mounting desire.

He has the softest touch I've ever felt. I know he's trying to control and restrain himself. His energy pulses with passion, same as mine. One downside to being 'special', apparently it's impossible to hide what you're truly feeling. Swallowing hard, I focus on the wall in front of me, desperately trying to reign in my more carnal thoughts.

The angel's hands grip my arms and turn me towards him. The towel catches on the side of the shower as I move and it pulls free, falling and exposing my breasts. Now all but pressing up against him. Nathaniel's eyes drop and his mouth parts. A flashing image burns through my mind of his soft lips kissing down my chest, it's so real I can almost feel his lips on my skin.

He jerks his eyes back up to mine, exhibiting an impressive degree of control, while I fix the towel. A part of me very strongly wishes he would exercise less control. I'm having such a hard time with my own needs I'd give myself over to him if he'd just make a move. The connection between Nathaniel and I is growing deeper. I need him. He relaxes only once the towel is back in place and I'm properly covered then he leans down and kisses my forehead.

"Let's finish getting you sorted," he says, a softness to his voice I've never heard before.

I nod, my heart thumping in my chest with a mix of anticipation and attraction.

"Yeah, let's do that," I say, my voice hoarse.

"Your arm, mademoiselle," he says playfully.

He draws looping ceremonial sigils with exquisite sweeps of his deft hands up and down my arms. He crouches in front of me, clasping my wrists in his hand, placing his lips directly over my arms. He speaks over the sigils that he's drawn in a tongue that seems familiar but again I can't quite put my finger on. I feel it activating something inside of me. A cold, burning fire races across my skin as the sigils ignite. I gasp, drawing a deep breath, and my eyes widen when I see I'm drawing energy straight from him into the sigils.

"Nathaniel!"

He rises and places a finger to his mouth. His eyes tell me to let it happen. A heartbeat later I stop drawing energy and the sigils blaze even brighter on my skin.

"They'll fade in time. I can't mark you all at once, but this will keep you from an unscheduled death. I'll be with you all the time, now, in some small way," he explains.

Something tells me that was already the case. Nathaniel, just like Efram and Rafe, was bound to me the moment our paths crossed. The connection between all of us is undeniable.

Holding my arms up, I watch as the sigils slowly fade, losing their brilliance. There's a delicate beauty to them that I find fascinating. My inspection is broken by the train car jerking. I'm thrown into Nathaniel, pressing him up against the wall. I'm acutely aware, once more, of how hard my nipples are and how much I want him.

We stare into each other's eyes as energy crackles between us. I rise onto my toes, our lips moving slowly towards each other. He leans in but just before our lips touch, he stiffens and jerks back, closing his eyes.

"We should get back to the others," he says.

I fall back on my feet. "Yeah," I sigh.

He steps out of the shower, hands me my clothes, then pulls the curtain closed. I know he's waiting out there, the perfect gentleman, exactly when I don't want him to be.

Shaking my head, I dress and emerge ready to face whatever comes next. All of the tension with the mages and now with Nathaniel too has been a great distraction from the fact that I still have a sense something bad is about to happen. Left with nothing else to focus on, that feeling is back. I follow Nathaniel through the train cars and back to the meal car where everyone else is waiting.

The moment we step into the car, I sense the weight in the air. Something has already happened. Rowan looks at me with sad eyes. The rest of the six purse their lips and avoid my gaze.

"What's going on?" I ask.

"We didn't just come here to help you," Ronan says, sitting at the head of the table, notably a safe distance from me.

"Okay?" I ask, suspicious.

"We have to take the seven with us," he continues.

"No," I say, shaking my head.

"Aviella, you should hear him out," Rafe says.

"No, why should I? He's crazy and I don't care," I say. "You of all people should get that."

"Aviella, our job is to protect the innocent," Ronan says. "Not just any innocent but those who will make a difference at the end times."

"In case you haven't noticed, we're in the end times," I retort.

"Not yet," Nathaniel says cryptically from behind me.

"Aviella, our entire order is formed for this single-purpose. We have been doing this for generations beyond count. They cannot go with you to Bunker 2. They will be safe with us. If they go, it could mean the end of everything. You have to believe me," Ronan pleads.

It doesn't matter that I feel the truth of his words, I don't want to believe them. Screw him and screw his ideas. I can't even look at him. I'm too angry, too hurt, so I stare at the floor, biting my lip. Rowan walks down the line and my stomach flips.

"Take the other six," I say, "if they want to go. Rowan stays with me."

The sadness on Rowan's face tells me everything I need to know. She reaches me and places her hand on my cheek in that gentle, soft way she has. She leans in until our foreheads are resting against each other. She wraps her arms around me and I can't hold back my tears.

"No, not you."

"We have to protect them. Their innocence and their powers will be needed," Ronan says. "You'll see each other again, for now they can't be put at risk. Their journey is not yours, they cannot go with you."

The four mages' energy pulses, mingling with my own and their blood calls to mine. They are familiar, they are safe. It makes me trust them. I don't want to, but I do. I know they're here to help but I don't want their help, not at this price.

Screw destiny and screw the fact that they're bound to me. It doesn't matter that it all feels connected. I tighten my arms around Rowan. "Please don't leave me."

She releases me and pushes me back, holding onto my shoulders. She kisses my forehead before turning and walking back to stand beside Ronan. It's all the signal I need, she doesn't need words to tell me she's going of her own free will.

"This sucks," I say. "How soon?"

"We can give you through dinner to say goodbye," Ronan answers.

"Great, how magnanimous of you."

Anita laughs, breaking the tension of the moment. Graham gets up and sets food out on the table as we start saying our goodbyes.

The dinner goes entirely too fast. I give each one a hug, making them swear that they'll stay safe and that we'll see each other again. I'm proud of the fact that I don't shed any tears until I get to Rowan and then I can't hold them back. She and I hold each other for a very long moment until at last she steps away. As she backs away, she mimes a heart-to-heart like she's saying I'll still be with you. I wipe furiously at my tears.

"Okay, you win," I say to Ronan. "Let's get this over with."

Luca and Killian don't waste time, kneeling and drawing sigils on the ground. The four mages take up positions around the markings and close their eyes. Their palms grow visibly red with magical heat. Their sculpted features make them look almost like they're performing a miracle as they weave magic. The air becomes heavy, almost damp with the energetic condensation of their magical intentions and soon a shimmering door to somewhere opens in the middle of the car. It's brilliant, shiny, right at the center of the mark. The mages herd the six through one at a time. An overwhelming sadness swells inside of me. It's hard to breathe, like a I can't catch my breath.

Rowan is last to go, she stops in the door and looks back at me. She blows me a kiss, hugs herself tightly and then throws her arms wide, tossing the hug to me then she steps through the door and disappears.

"I know this is hard," Ronan says as the other mages step through the door. "It really is for the best."

I shake my head, unable to speak. The mage nods like he understands, but there's no way he can. The empty hole in my chest aches, throbbing with the loss of Rowan.

Screw what's best, I want my friend.

# CHAPTER TWENTY-TWO

The mages' magic fades and a heavy silence falls across the train car. Staring at the spot where the door was, my limbs feel too heavy to move. An empty blackness wells up within me.

Rowan's gone. I'm alone. Again.

Efram and Rafe stand next to me but don't speak. Nathaniel walks over to the magical symbols on the floor and kneels, placing his fingers on them. He nods, as if somehow satisfied, and then rises. He goes over to a small sink and wets a cloth. Going back to the symbols he scrubs, washing them off the floor. Efram clears his throat and squeezes past me to help Nathaniel.

Rafe stays close. I sense his concern and that he wants to help, maybe embrace me, or something. I can't have that right now. Rowan was my heart and I don't know if I'll ever see her again.

Watching Nathaniel work, my thoughts turn to my father. I haven't felt so alone since he and I were separated. Efram looks up from his work, catching my eye he gives a half smile. The connection between the two of us pulses with an easy, soft rhythm. It helps, a little. Sighing, I turn my back on them and pour myself a drink of water.

What if I lose them too?

A cold chill runs down my spine and I shiver. I hadn't thought about that before. Of course, losing Rowan was another thing I'd never considered. Goosebumps race down my arms and my knees shake. I grab onto the counter and steady myself. It's hard to get a breath, I'm gasping, desperately trying. Strong hands grip my shoulders, supporting me. Bowing my head, I can't hold it in, I'm sobbing like a baby. Rafe tightens his grip and turns me, pulling me into an embrace.

Wrapping my arms around him, I give over to my emotions. The throbbing, empty ache of loss pounds inside, letting it out is my only option. I'm acutely aware of Efram and Nathaniel's eyes on me without having to look. Their concern is palpable, and their energies pass over me, caressing my skin with gentle, worried touches. It's reassuring.

"I can't lose you guys," I say, my tears finally running dry.

"We're not going anywhere," Rafe says, his voice soft next to my ear.

Nodding, I straighten and wipe away the last of my tears, trying to regain some sense of composure.

"I have a book you might enjoy," Efram offers.

"Thanks."

I don't think I can focus on a book right now. My thoughts are scattered and continuously circling back around to the loss of Rowan, but it is sweet of him to offer.

"We could do some karaoke," Rafe jokes. "I'd be happy to sing for you."

"I appreciate it," I say, meaning it. "But I think I'm going to take a shower."

The three men exchange a quick glance with each other.

Rafe's jaw tightens almost imperceptibly before he nods. I don't know what to make of that.

"Of course," he says. "That's an excellent idea."

I walk towards the back of the car, feeling their eyes on me. With one hand on the door between the cars, I bite my lip and consider what I'm about to say.

"I appreciate you guys," I say. "I can't imagine going through this without you."

I don't wait for any replies before stepping through the door.

Now that we're seven people less, I don't worry about conserving hot water. Turning it on full blast, I stand and let it beat down. Tension washes out of my muscles but does nothing for the empty hole where Rowan should be.

*Let it go, Aviella. She's safe, safer than you are.*

The truth of my words helps more than anything else has. We're heading for Bunker 2, a mega-bunker, which brings all its own baggage to worry about. That's not even considering the dead things that are chasing me. Or the thing that tried to drain my energy, whatever that was. Considering all that, Rowan is better off far away from me. My desire to have her close is purely selfish.

*Well that makes sense. Either I really care about my friend and I can try to be happy she's safe, or as safe as anyone can be in the apocalypse with a new trumpet about to sound, or I can be a selfish-jerk and pout about the fact that she's not going into danger with me.*

*What's it going to be Aviella?*

Shaking my head, I let the water run across my face and come to terms with my own fears and loss. Fear. That's what it really is. Fear of being alone again. Part of me is still that little girl waiting in the apartment for my father to come and save me. Scared, alone, and desperate.

Time to grow up. No matter how much it sucks. I let out

a long sigh and stand in the water until it starts to turn cool. After ringing out my hair out, I reach outside the curtain and grab a towel to wrap around myself then step out. The mirrors are steamed over from my long shower. Wiping it clear with a hand, I stare at my reflection. The bags under my eyes show my lack of sleep. I'm pale, tired looking, but I'm alive.

This is it Aviella. Destiny has called, and you have to answer.

Is it always like this? Did any of us so called 'specials' have a choice? Or is everything playing out according to some greater plan? If it is, then it sucks. Who wrote a plan where the entire world must go to hell to get to... what? Some bright tomorrow? Surely this can't be all there is. There has to be something more, something we are working towards.

Nathaniel and the mages have all hinted at some greater plan, some goal we're working towards. That feels right. It resonates in my blood, if nothing else it gives me much needed hope. Hope that everything will work out, somehow.

I run my fingers through my hair, trying to give it some semblance of a style before stepping out of the shower stalls. Looking myself over one last time, I walk out and bump into Efram.

"Oh, excuse me," I say, stepping back.

"It's fine," he replies.

His eyes linger just below my face, taking in the beaded water on my exposed skin. My cheeks flush hot and warmth pools between my thighs. The connection between the two of us pulses alive with suppressed desire.

When he looks away, I feel it, like his eyes are being torn off my skin. He swallows hard. It's not just my desire in the connection. His is every bit as strong.

"May I?" he asks, motioning at my arm where Nathaniel's sigils are exposed.

I nod, raising my arm so he can see. Sparks jump between our skin when he takes my hand in his and a shock rocks through me. Our two energies intertwine, melding together. The way his jaw tightens, feels it too.

He inspects the angel's mark, tracing it with his eyes where it goes up and across me.

"At least he's kept unjust death from you," he says. "That should make things easier. There are other sigils you should take on – when we have more time."

His fingers graze across my skin, drawing heat to the surface. Our eyes meet and I see him struggling to resist our chemistry.

"Yeah," I breathe, my mouth and throat dry.

"I'll never let anything happen to you, you know that, right?"

The moment stretches. I can't take my eyes off his lips, like I'm watching the words emerge, but I'm consumed with wondering what they would taste like. I want to feel his lips on my skin, exploring me. His strong arms wrapped around me, holding me tight.

"I know," I exhale.

Desire is a magnet pulling us towards each other and I'm not sure we can resist. My willpower is crumbling and as it does, the towel slips. I should care, but I don't. I lean in closer, unable to stop the attraction.

"Aviella," he says, and my name on his lips ignites the fire inside, making it a raging inferno.

My heart pounds and my limbs are weak.

He steps back, and the moment is broken. Averting his eyes, he shakes his head. I know he's struggling within himself through the connection we have.

"No, not now," he says, his voice barely more than a whisper.

I understand. He's right, now is not the time to be exploring personal desires. There's too much at stake.

"I've got your back too," I say, trying to change the subject to something more relevant.

"Thank you."

He turns and leaves the car without another word. Alone, I dress and take a few minutes to contemplate what just happened.

"THAT WAS A GOOD MOVE," RAFE SAYS.

"Thank you," Efram replies.

I mark my place in the book I'm reading with a finger and watch as the two of them spar. They've moved aside the furniture from the middle of the car to give themselves some room. I have to admit, if only to myself, it's made more interesting by the fact that they're both shirtless. The sheen of sweat across their hard bodies ignites strong interest.

They're using wooden practice swords. Rafe attacks with quick, precise strikes that reminds me of a snake. His motions are a blur and I'm impressed that Efram manages to counter most of them. They circle each other, swords held ready before them, each man looking for an opening.

Efram's sword starts to swing in from Rafe's right, but as soon as Rafe moves to block, Efram switches directions, swinging around and coming in from the left. Rafe leaps to one side and with a blindingly fast movement, he catches the attack. The swords clash together with a loud clack.

My heart races in my chest. Can I achieve such speed and accuracy? Rafe is like the perfect predator. His eyes don't miss a thing. His motions are so precise, so exact, it's like he knows ahead of time where to place the sword before he ever moves.

Efram is more methodical and calculating. His motions are less fluid looking than Rafe's. It's more like he's planning ahead with careful thought and insight rather than reacting to the ever-changing action.

They're breathing heavily, focused on their practice, setting aside words in favor of action. I enjoy the silence. Watching them allows me to have a focus that I've found hard to maintain since Rowan left.

They clash again, Efram darting in and this time his sword connects with Rafe's left leg. Rafe winces as he dances back. Red pulses through his aura, the only sign he gives of the pain.

Everything can turn that fast. A split second and it all changes. Before that hit, I would've said Rafe was winning. This is what our life is now. At any moment everything can change, my best friend can leave. The probability is high that any moment can bring another life-changing experience. It's a heavy thought.

"Okay," Rafe says, lowering his sword.

"Is that all?" Efram asks, a grin on his face.

"I should relieve Nathaniel," Rafe says. "You can continue your practice with him."

Rafe manages to leave the car without a limp, which I find impressive. That last hit was hard. In a moment Nathaniel enters the car. He and Efram lock eyes with each other and the challenge is issued. Silently Nathaniel nods and unbuttons his shirt.

Nathaniel is ridiculously ripped. He could be the cover model for one of my favorite romance novels. The angel rolls his shoulders and then does a couple of deep knee bends, stretching himself out. He takes up the wooden sword and drops into a defensive position in front of Efram. His eyes take on a faraway look, like he's not really there, his thoughts consumed with something else.

In my mind I lay odds on Efram beating him. Efram raises the sword and then lowers it before dropping into his own ready stance. The two men stare at each other and then there's a blur as they clash. The swords are flying so fast I can barely follow them. Their blur in my vision and even the sound of them clacking is delayed, by the time it reaches my ears they've hit three or four more times.

Nathaniel moves with grace and power. Efram has more of a staccato feel to his motions. He's less predictable but in an exacting way. It's like he's mastered a quantum rhythm with his movements. His is an accuracy that's neither angelic nor demon, yet still a formidable opponent all the same.

Efram tags Nathaniel first and I let out a cheerful yelp. Efram glances at me, smiles, then bows, tipping his sword. The angel looks mildly surprised, but nods then resets into a ready position. The two men clash again, and I relax, enjoying the spectacle. Before either can land another hit, the train slows. Jumping to my feet, I go into the conductor's booth.

Rafe stands at the pump but isn't working it. The former slaves are huddled at the back of the car behind him. Ahead is a flashing red light and there's a barrier built over the tracks. Turning his head, Rafe looks at me and makes a motion across his throat, indicating I should stop the car.

I look at the controls and pull back on the lever that I think controls the speed. My assumption is right and the train grinds to a halt as Nathaniel and Efram join me.

"What is this?" Efram asks.

"I don't know," I say.

Out of the corner my eye I watch Nathaniel tighten his jaw, but he doesn't say anything. The train slows to a halt. Rafe jumps off the car and walks up to the barrier. The three of us watch from the conductor's booth as he looks it over. Once he's finished he returns and climbs up into the car.

"We could clear it," Rafe says. "But it's going to take some time."

There are shouts outside of the railcar before any of us speak. Heart pounding in my chest, I look outside and see armed men rushing us. There are dozens of them and all of them have automatic weapons. The four of us exchange a look.

"Don't resist," Nathaniel says.

"Who the hell is it?" Efram asks.

"Bunker 2 security," he answers, shaking his head.

"All of you, step out with your hands in the air," a deep, booming voice orders.

We exchange one last glance but there aren't any options. Rafe leads the way and the rest of us follow. The security team are dressed in full riot gear, like a SWAT team from before the apocalypse. They push us around until we're in a line, up against the car. At least six of them have their guns trained on us always. A very tall and large figure steps out from behind the guards. He takes off his helmet and my breath catches in my chest.

It's a Dragon.

His perfect, sharp chiseled features are accented by dark, wavy hair that curls past his ears. His eyes are deep, copper pools that take in everything. His aura is a pulsing red that I've never seen before in a human. Dragon-shifters were the fabled four horsemen.

He makes a motion, waving his hand in the air. Two men step out of the guard line and approach. They pull cuffs out of their belts and silently stare, waiting, until we raise our hands and let them put them on. As soon as the steel clasps around my wrists my magic is shut off from me. I look from the cuffs over to Efram, fear eating at me.

"It's Nusteel," he whispers.

I haven't heard of this before. Handcuffs that cut off

magic? Suddenly I'm a lot more scared than I was. I look over at Rafe and I see the wheels turning behind his eyes. There are too many of them. We don't have a choice but to comply.

"You're being taken into custody pending interrogation," the Dragon says, his wide, full lips turned down in disapproval. "We want to know your part in the fall of Bunker E274."

"We're survivors not perpetrators," Rafe protests.

The cold gaze of the Dragon sweeps over the demon like he's only just noticed the other exists.

"That's to be determined," he says.

Tears prick my eyes as we're separated. Four guards take each of us, weapons trained and ready. They force march us past the barrier on the track and up to a set of massive double doors that look like they're made of reinforced concrete.

The Dragon stands at the lead, staring at the doors and as if by his will, they silently swing open. It doesn't take a lot of pushing for them to get us moving and we're marched through dark tunnels until we come out into an open space.

The four of us huddle together, waiting to see what happens next. Two men rush up to the Dragon and whisper something I can't hear. He nods sharply and makes quick motions with his hands. One of the guards jabs his gun into my ribs, pushing me.

"Ow," I exclaim.

"If you hurt her..." Rafe says, not finishing his sentence.

The Dragon turns his cold gaze on Rafe, saying nothing. The guard jabs me again and I stumble into motion, herded towards a door. Looking over my shoulder before I step through, I see my friends are being led to separate rooms. I try to catch each of their gazes. We'll be back together again, soon. We have to be.

# CHAPTER TWENTY-THREE

The interview process drags on for what feels like forever. I sit across from the pensive looking man for hours as he asks the same mundane questions over and over. They're variations on a theme, wanting to know what happened in bunker E247 and what part I had in it.

I lie through my teeth, hoping the rest of the boys are doing the same. It doesn't seem like a smart idea to say what my true role in it was. Probably not the best way to be welcomed into a new bunker by saying 'hey the admin of the previous one I lived in summoned a demonic army of undead and sent them after me.'

Great opening line it is not.

Thinking about the guys, I hope they're okay. I was nervous, expecting something much darker and more sinister than an endless series of questions. I assume the boys are being treated the same. What I don't understand is why these people are so concerned with E247. They have to know that this type of thing has happened before and will surely happen again.

He shifts more papers in front of himself, picking them

up then tapping them on the table, making sure they're square. He sets the stack back down and looks over his notes. He tsk's a couple of times and shakes his head. He's done that multiple times to the point of being completely annoying.

"So, tell me again," he says, looking up from the papers. "How do you know the admin was dabbling in 'bad things' as you put it."

I sigh and do my best not to roll my eyes. Tapping my fingers on the table, I meet his eyes and prepare to give the lie again.

"Because," I say, smiling. "Like I said the last fifty times, I saw him walking among the undead and they weren't attacking him. Therefore, I assume he was in league with them."

He stares at me with hard, cold eyes, unperturbed by the heavy sarcasm in my voice. I try to meet his stare without looking away but there's something so empty about him I flinch first.

"Interesting," he says, not for the first time.

He looks over my shoulder at the camera in the corner. I don't know if somebody up there is signaling him somehow or what but it's not the first time he's done that either.

He gathers up the papers again but this time he slides them all into a file folder. He squares them carefully, making very sure the corners are precisely aligned. Once he's satisfied with that, he closes the folder, letting it sit in front of him, and rests his hands on top of each other on it.

"That will be the end of our interview," he says. "You have been cleared of any wrongdoing. Your story is in line with the reports from the field team we sent to check on the condition of the bunker."

I stare with my mouth agape. They knew this the entire time?

"Were there any survivors?" I ask, pushing past my annoyance.

"Bunker E247 has been decommissioned," he says cryptically.

"That's not an answer."

"Bunker E247 has been decommissioned," he repeats, making it clear I'll get no further answers.

"What about my friends?"

"They've also been cleared," he says. "They are currently pending assignment."

"I'm not sure what that means."

"There are no free rides in Bunker 2," he says. "Everybody has a job."

Great. That doesn't leave me much hope. Nathaniel said it was much different here and I'm beginning to understand. We've only just arrived and already it feels more like a prison than a home. I'm positive it's not going to be easy to make my way back to my friends.

The interrogator stands up and waits, staring at me. I take the hint and rise as well. Silently he motions towards the door then walks behind me. Outside there are two security personnel waiting. One of them steps over and puts my cuffs back on.

"Seriously?" I ask.

No one bothers to answer me. Sighing, I resign myself to the situation. The security guards stand on either side of me, lightly resting a hand on each of my arms. They guide me away from the interview room and out through a series of tunnels. It doesn't take long before they stop before a door and punch in a code. There's the sound of a lock turning as the other one removes my cuffs. The door swings open and they step to either side, letting me walk through.

Only when the door closes do I realize they didn't come inside with me. Blinking and feeling grateful, I look around my new surroundings. It's a library! Rows and rows of shelves are filled floor to ceiling with books. It's like they dropped me off in heaven.

"Hello?" I call.

No one answers so I walk over to the first row of stacks and run my fingers along the spines. I love the feel of old books under my fingertips. They're a rarity and to see so many of them in one place makes my heart skip a beat. It's a beautiful thing. Selecting one at random, I pull it off the shelf and hold it in my hands. The weight of it, the smell, and the feel of the leather cover transports me to another place.

"Good choice," a rich baritone voice says from behind me.

Startled, I yelp and spin around with an apology on my lips. It dies the moment I see him. He has black hair with silver at the temples, cut short on the sides but thick and curly on top. A week's worth of growth adorns his face, accenting his strong jaw and giving him an air of distinction. His brown eyes are warm and deeply intelligent. He's dressed in a dark gray suit with a white shirt but no tie. His shirt is unbuttoned on the top three buttons, revealing perfectly tanned skin.

As soon as I see him, I feel my energy waver. It's like I'm looking at him through heat waves rising from hot asphalt. Everything swims but I pull myself back into focus. There's a definite connection between us, a pull, not dissimilar to what I felt when I first met Efram.

Pushing that aside, more than anything, he's the key to finding my friends.

"Aviella? I'm Silas. I'll be your—"

"Where are my friends?" I ask, going on the attack.

"They're in pre-assignment interviews, now."

"What does that even mean?" I ask, not relenting.

"It means exactly what I said," he says, unperturbed by my tone.

"I need to see them. Now."

"Aviella—"

"No, no don't do that, I've waited long enough. I need to see my friends now. I need to know that they're okay."

Suddenly his energy becomes much more imposing, dominating, it's like he's bigger or more in my space even though he hasn't moved. He squares his shoulders and his jaw tightens.

"No," he says.

I open my mouth to protest but no sound comes out. There's a commanding presence to him that wasn't there before. He seems completely unfazed by my rebelliousness.


"Let us start, again," he says, his voice rich and cultured. Every word is carefully considered before he speaks it. "My name is Silas, I will be your sponsor, your trainer, and your ally."

When he says ally, something pulses in my blood. I have the same connection to him as I do with Efram, Rafe and Nathaniel. Through it comes trust and a strong desire to help.

"Okay," I agree.

I sense how keenly he wants me to believe in him. My new mentor holds a hand out and I take it. The moment our skin touches an image blooms in my mind. Another trumpet sounds, serpent tail steeds storm across the land, herding screaming masses before them. I gasp, jerking my hand back. Silas meets my eyes levelly.

"Trouble is coming and there isn't much time. Your blood sings of destiny, I know what you are, let me help and I will prepare you."

I don't think anything else could make it clearer that he's here to guide me. Whatever greater force seems to be running my life, he's a part of it. His energy feels like it's inside of me after that vision. His presence is... too much. Especially after losing contact with Rowan and the guys.

"There's a process here. You need to relax and let it happen. There's more than locust swarms to be wary of in the world," Silas says.

Right. Well, cooperate or what? With my distinct lack of options, I decide to so as he asks, after all what choice do I have?

I DON'T HAVE ANY IDEA WHAT TIME IT IS, A COMMON PROBLEM living in the bunkers, but I do know I'm exhausted. The interrogation process seemed like it took forever and quite likely it did. Silas shows me around the library, making it clear that I can explore at will. Before we're finished I'm yawning despite my best efforts to suppress it.

"You must be exhausted," he says.

I nod, yawning yet again. He leads the way through the stacks to the back of the library. There are several doors and he moves to one, pushing it open and stepping aside. It's a small sleeping area with a bed that looks so comfortable I could cry.

"Go ahead and sleep," he says. "I'll be waiting when you wake up."

I'm too tired to argue. I go to the bed and I'm asleep before my head hits the pillow.

I'M DREAMING. I KNOW IT'S A DREAM. IT'S THAT WEIRD sensations when you wake up inside the dream and you know it's a dream, but you can't get out of it. I'm being pushed through the sky by some power that I can't see and there are rings of light that I pass through as I fly. It's like being in a videogame. Each time I go through one of the rings, my power surges.

My skin tingles as the reserves of my energy pool become deeper. Each time one of the bright, golden rings approaches, it's like time slows and then as I pass through, it speeds up incredibly fast only to slow again when I reach the other side. I have no idea what's going on, but it seems like so much more than a dream.

"Aviella," Silas' rich baritone voice calls to me from a long distance.

I try to answer but I can't. I see him in front of me which is weird because it's like his face is overlaid on top of the scene I'm flying through. Maybe it's more like I'm seeing two things at once. I see the room behind him, the one I went to sleep in, but I also see the sky and the rings speeding by me. I'm not sure which one is real.

The concern in Silas' eyes is real. His hand reaches towards me and I have to suppress a laugh. I wonder if he can catch me because I'm flying through these rings so quick.

He grabs my shoulder with a firm, yet gentle grip. The moment he does, I jerk awake, lying on the cot with blankets and sheets twisted around me. Cold sweat breaks out across me as I look around, wide-eyed and panting.

"What in the holy hell was that?" I ask.

"A time distortion loop," Silas replies, as if that answers anything.

"Yeah ok, sure. Is that a good or a bad thing?"

"We'll see," he replies. "Come with me please."

He leads the way out of my room to another office dominated by a massive desk and sparse furniture. He motions that I should take the seat in front of the desk while he goes around behind it.

"I'd like to run a few tests on you."

"What kind of tests?" I ask, wondering if he intends to stick me with lots of needles or what.

"Simple ones," he says. "Designed to give me a read on your body and abilities."

"Well that sounds dirty," I flirt.

No smile, not even a hint of one. He's as bad as Nathaniel. Clearing his throat, he pulls a deck of cards over. Waiting until I've given him my full attention, he lifts one of the cards and shows it to me. It has a weird symbol that I don't recognize but the moment I look, strange words pour out of me. I have no idea what I say but he nods and sets the card to side, apparently satisfied.

He continues doing similar test for the next hour. Sometimes I speak in tongues I don't recognize and other times my power surges, but nothing happens. Each time something happens within me he nods and has a knowing look. Good for him, I wish I knew what was going on.

"Your blood is ancient, Aviella," he says at last. "You've tested much higher than most."

"Hurray?" I comment. "What does that mean?"

"It will award you a lot of access to what the bunker to has to offer."

"Will it let me see my friends?"

"Eventually," he says. "First we have to train you. You need to increase control over your powers."

"Thank you, Captain Obvious," I quip, but again get no rise out of him. "Will they be okay?"

"I'll make sure that they are," he answers. "Now, let's begin."

So much for wasting time. We set to work and I do my best to be a good student. Largely, I'm hoping by getting through this phase quickly I can reconnect with Rafe, Nathaniel, and Efram.

Hours turn into days as we train. From the moment I wake up to the moment I fall asleep, usually with my nose in a book, I'm studying or practicing. He wants me to learn ceremonial magic first. It's a lot of fancy rites and what seems like pompous extras added on to just doing some damn magic. As the days pass, my trust in Silas grows.

So does my attraction to him.

His intelligence is through the roof. I've never felt in awe of anybody before but the power reserves he has, combined with his encyclopedic knowledge of all things magical, is inspiring.

It doesn't hurt that he's totally gorgeous. One time when he was instructing me, he stood so close I could count his thick eyelashes and got super distracted by how pretty they were and how intense his eyes looked when he was speaking. Needless to say, he chided me on not paying attention to what he was teaching.

At some point during the week he has a tailor come and measure me for new clothes. I've never had custom fitted clothes before and when they arrive I spend a few hours trying them on. There's a warped mirror in my room which I enjoy looking at myself in with all the new outfits.

"Very nice," Silas says from the door.

My cheeks heat at being caught admiring myself. Looking at the floor, I manage to stammer out, "thank you."

He moves towards me and lifts my face. "You have nothing to be ashamed of," he murmurs. He lifts my arm and spins me and I laugh, enjoying the way my skirt flares out. I give Silas a curtsey and it brings a smile to his face. I feel like a Princess.

A loud knock echoes through the library cutting the moment short. Silas turns on one heel and disappears. A sensation of something about to happen crawls across my skin like a cool breeze. I don't know what but I know it's not going to be great.

In a few moments Silas returns, looking grim with his brow furrowed. "We have to prepare you, quickly," he says.

"For what?"

"Your presence has been requested at a social mixer."

"Sounds fancy, buuut," I drag the word out, "I'm guessing from the look on your face this is a bad thing?"

"Perhaps," he says.

"Then turn it down, I won't go."

Probably best if I don't mention what happened last time I was invited to a party. I mentally cringe and vow never to drink wine again.

"That's not an option," he says grimly. "The best I can do is prepare you to swim in very dangerous waters."

Great, right when I thought things were about to become bearable. As I've come to expect from Silas he wastes no time. Instead of focusing on controlling my powers, now it's all about etiquette. We have less than a day to prepare. I thought learning magic was hard and overwhelming but now I relish the idea of going back to it.

"Never show weakness," he admonishes.

"What did I do?"

"You looked to the side."

"Seriously? That's all I did wrong?"

He doesn't answer me with words and doesn't have to. His look says it all. Sighing and rolling my eyes, I try again. I have to do better. I don't have time to get this right, but I can't be wrong. It's ridiculous. Every motion, every glance, even the intonation of every word I say is apparently going to be measured, weighed, and evaluated against some scale that I can't even begin to comprehend. And I only have hours to learn all of this.

"It will have to do," Silas says at last.

I plop down in an overstuffed chair with a feeling of relief. I didn't know that purely mental activities could leave me feeling so exhausted.

"How much time do we have?" I ask.

"Time enough for you to change your clothes," he replies. "Then we have to go."

"Great," I say. "Just what I wanted to hear."

He doesn't bother responding to my sarcasm. Silas is always perfect, cultured, and above entering such vulgar frays. I wonder what he would be like if he ever let his jeweled cufflinks loose. Sometimes I catch a look that lingers just a little too long or a feeling in his energy. It's rare though, he's very good at hiding his feelings.

"I'll bring you a selection of dresses," he says.

I take the hint that I'm dismissed and go to my room, preparing by stripping down to my underwear. Silas knocks at my door and I look out through the crack. He has four different dresses hooked on his fingers. His eyes narrow the moment he sees me through the small opening of the door and there's an instant that something pulses through the energy connection between us. He resumes his composure almost immediately, pointedly looking to the side.

I can't resist the urge to be mischievous, so I throw the door open wide and stand exposed in front of him. He holds the dresses out at arm's length and pointedly stares at the wall to the right.

"Which one do you like best?" I tease.

"I suggest the blue," he says, still not looking.

"Okay," I say, taking all four dresses in and slowly shutting the door.

Once the door closes I can't suppress a giggle. It serves him right and it's fun to see him lose a little bit of that perfect composure.

I ended up choosing the blue dress to please Silas. It has an old roman feel to it, with light fabric that drapes over my shoulders and flows down to my ankles, belted with a slim tie at the waist. I hold Silas' arm just as he taught me. He navigates us through the crowd of people, introducing us only to the correct ones. There's an art to this that I barely comprehend. Some people who attempt to talk to us he absolutely ignores while others he forces to engage with us. I do my best to remember their names, but it quickly becomes a blur. So many perfect faces, beautiful smiles, and clothes that are worth more than all the clothing combined in the orphanage I grew up in.

As we step away from the latest couple that Silas introduced me to, I spot Efram. He's seated at a table at the back of the room and looks well. A loud, pushy woman sits in front of him. She's so beautiful it's almost painful to look at her. Perfect skin, not a hair out of place, and her sleeveless dress dives down in the back almost to her ass. She has her hand held out and he's holding it in both of his. My stomach clenches tight seeing him with her.

"You're not very good at this," she says snootily.

"Yes ma'am," Efram says, grimacing.

I can imagine the train of thoughts going in his head, or maybe what I hope he's thinking. She's so arrogant he can't possibly find her attractive, right? It's apparent he's been set up to do readings. According to Silas, everything in this bunker is about the push for excellence. The rich want psychic readings that tell them how to get an edge over their rivals.

"Silas, who is this guest you brought?" a new man asks.

"Allow me to introduce Aviella," Silas intones.

Forcing myself to quit staring at Efram I turn and hold

my hand out daintily, like Silas has taught me, and put on my best smile. I don't meet the man's eyes, that would be inviting too much. Instead, I stare at his shoulders and pointedly ignore the two women on either side of him, both of which are dressed rather trashily. The man himself is obviously well cultured and very rich. When he takes my hand, his fingernails are perfectly manicured. Slowly he raises my hand to his lips which are dry and papery.

"A pleasure," he says.

I don't bother answering with words, instead I giggle, another thing Silas encouraged me to do. Giggling, seriously? If this was any other situation I would never giggle. What am I? Some stupid airhead? A too stupid to live heroine in a bad romance? It turns my stomach playing this role.

"We'll have to get together later," the man says.

"Of course," Silas says, quickly guiding me away.

"I see Efram, where are Rafe and Nathaniel?" I whisper.

"I couldn't control where they were placed, only that they weren't put at the bottom of the heap," he says.

I nod in understanding. There's nothing more that I could ask for, at least I know they're safe. We continue making our way around the gathering but at one point I notice an open door draped with purple cloth. People are going in and out of it and I wonder what's on the other side.

"What is that?" I ask Silas.

He follows the direction of my gaze and his frown deepens. He leads us towards it and we step through. Inside, my breath is taken away. A cage dominates the middle of the room surrounded by the overdressed attendees of this mixer. They cheer, waving money in the air, all blocking my view of what's happening in the cage. Silas stiffens then turns back towards the door we came in.

My stomach sinks and that sense of something being wrong washes over me. It's all I can do to keep my composure. Tightening my grip on Silas's arm, I glare at him. A slight tensing of his jaw is the only response he gives. Taking a deep breath, I remember the training Silas has given me. Give away nothing. If anyone notices it could expose me, creating a new weakness.

"What is this?" I whisper, glaring at him.

"Fighting cages," he says, his voice barely over a mumble.

"Fighting?" I ask, horrified, my stomach flipping over and bile rising in my throat.

His energy has a tension that flows towards a resolve. He weaves us through the crowd of people around the cage, deftly working us in and out. Underlying the cheering comes the clacking of wood against wood. It reminds me of watching the boys spar.

Stepping around a woman with the most enormous head-dress I've ever seen, a monstrosity of feathers and flowers woven together in a god-awful conglomeration of I don't know what, I see inside the cage for the first time. I gasp as my stomach tightens, feeling like I've been punched.

Rafe is fighting inside the cage against a man who's at least twice as big as him. They're armed with only wooden swords but it's still obviously dangerous. Rafe is shirtless and there's a dark bruise on the left side of his chest.

"Get him out of there!" I hiss.

The bigger man attacks, swinging overhead with both hands, a crushing blow if ever there was one. It looks like Rafe will take the hit but at the last moment he moves, dodging under the blow and striking his opponent in the stomach. The loud echo of the wooden sword against flesh is followed by the cheering of the crowd.

A referee steps into the cage. He goes to Rafe and takes his left hand raising it in the air. A mix of cheers and curses rise from the crowd. Rafe stares straight ahead, looking resigned. He's alive, that's what matters, right? I try to reassure myself with that fact.

"I can't," Silas answers.

Bile rises into my mouth and I have to swallow it down hard. Can't. Can't help my friend. I reach out towards Rafe with my power, caressing him. His head jerks and he focuses on me. His familiar, ironic grin spreads across his face.

"Stop that," Silas hisses, tightening his grip on my arm.

"What?" I ask.

"They'll sense it," he says.

"I have to..."

"No, you don't. He's fine and there is Nathaniel, he's up next. These are not to the death. It's a good job for them."

White hot anger pounds through my blood leaving me shaking. He's wrong and I want to prove it but I can't do anything. The last time I lost it at a party, an entire bunker died. I can't do that again.

Rafe has a bruise that looks very bad. I don't doubt there are much worse jobs he could be stuck into but this is awful. Looking past Rafe, I spot Nathaniel and he looks okay as well.

Damn it.

Breathing through the anger, I regain my composure the best I can.

"Silas," a deep bass voice rumbles behind us.

Silas turns us around, tearing my eyes away from my friends.

Veiled and poised, I remind myself.

All my thoughts are pushed away when I see the man whose voice interrupted me. There are two of them standing side by side, and they literally ooze sex appeal. My heart stutters in my chest and I forget to breathe. They're perfection made flesh. As different from each other as two people could be yet both are truly perfect.

When they look at me I feel transparent, like their eyes are undressing me. There's an unbelievable amount of magnetism in their auras. Instinctively I scan them with my power. There are layers to them, so many layers acting as a shield against the world. Hiding who and what they really are, their true intentions. Still, beyond the many layered shields of social veneer that they're hiding behind, I feel their hearts.

I look at them for a long, breathless moment before I realize they're Dragons. One is the same, dark haired who captured me and my friends weeks ago.

"Unfortunately, our cousins are running late," the one I've never seen before says. "You'll have to excuse them." He is slim and not quite six feet tall with long, black hair that hangs nearly to his waist. His skin is the color of aged ivory and his eyes slant almost delicately at the corners. There is nothing feminine about him however, he exudes confident, masculine sex appeal.

It feels like my energy is caught by theirs in a dancing web, weaving in and out and through. I couldn't stop them if I tried. They each take one of my hands, lifting it to their lips, their eyes never leaving mine. Warmth burns where their lips touch my skin. My core tightens, and I'm almost overcome with desire that comes raging out of nowhere.

I wonder if all Dragons drip sex like these two?

As if in answer to my question, two more men walk up and join us.

"Ah, they've arrived," the same dragon as before says. "Allow me to introduce us. This is Tynan and Casimir."

He motions to the two newcomers. I hold my hand out to them and they take it in turn, pressing their lips to my skin and creating the same effect on my body.

"A pleasure," I say, breathless, heart pounding in my chest so loud they must be able to hear it.

"This is my brother Alaric and I am Shen," he says.

I've heard stories about the Dragons, rumors, myths and lies. No one knows the truth, but I know there's something here, in these men, that I'm looking for. Maybe even something I'm destined to have. One thing is for sure, my life just became a lot more complicated.

# CHAPTER TWENTY-FOUR

*I*t's been three weeks since we attended the mixer. The Dragons scare me and I'm thankful that I haven't had to deal with them again. The power they have is frightening enough, but the attraction to them is even scarier. When I'm in their presence it pounds against me like a siren's call. I don't know what part they play in my future, but I do know there will be more between us.

Looking up from the book I'm reading, I rub my weary eyes. Silas is a nonstop taskmaster. Quietly demanding and pushing me to study more. I'm sick to death of looking at complex rituals. My days have been split between studying books and practicing what I've learned.

"Have you finished Kunin's Dissertation on Sigils?" Silas asks.

"Yes," I say, exasperation clear in my voice. "I'm also well into Boone's Guide to Magical Creatures."

"Good," he says.

Closing the book, I stand and stretch. I'm mentally exhausted but it's hard to keep my thoughts from Rafe and Nathaniel. I'm worried all the time. Are they okay? Is one of them hurt? Are they surviving? How do I get them out of the fighting cages?

"I'm taking a shower," I say.

Silas arches an eyebrow but says nothing. That's good enough. I leave him sitting at the tables and head for the small shower at the back of the library.

I take my time with the shower because here in Bunker 2 there seems to be a lot more hot water than anywhere else I've lived. I figure I might as well enjoy it. When I emerge, I'm refreshed and ready to confront sticking my nose into a book for hours. I wrap a towel around myself and head for my bunk, but when I step out of the bathroom Silas is standing right there.

My skin immediately flushes and I feel his eyes on my exposed cleavage. Anticipation makes my mouth dry. I get a wild impulse to drop the towel but I resist. I seem to be having these almost naked oops moments too frequently lately. Silas' desire, no matter how restrained and refined, is palpable between the two of us.

Dutifully he turns his back on me. "I apologize," he says.

Ever the gentleman, his restraint makes me want him more. Longing throbs at the apex of my thighs and I take a step forward before I can stop myself. No, wait. I can't rush this. How could I get intimate with Silas when Efram is miserable and Nathaniel and Rafe are in danger? Images of each of them flash through my thoughts, even the mages and the Dragons vie for a place in my mind. Oh my God, the Dragons, the thought of them does nothing to calm my carnal desires.

Silas clears his throat and I get a grip on myself. I've grown very fond of him in such a short time. I wonder what it would be like if he ever let himself relax. I imagine he would be gentle, dutiful and treat me like a princess. I enjoy his matter-of-fact manner and his deadpan humorous way of stating the obvious.

He makes a quick glance over his shoulder. "I will step out," he says. "Let you get dressed."

"Yeah," I agree. "Good idea."

He steps out of the room and I exhale a breath I didn't know I was holding. My heart slows in my chest and the flush lessens. Catching my breath, I dress quickly, not wanting to keep him waiting.

"What's up?" I ask.

He reaches into a pocket and pulls out a piece of paper, holding it up between the two of us. When he meets my eyes, his brow furrows.

"Your friends have been entered into a tournament. We've been invited to come watch."

"What kind of tournament?" I ask.

He frowns deeper and inhales a sharp breath. "A bloody one. You'll need to keep your composure, like I've shown you."

I swallow down my nerves, trying to not assume the worst.

"When?" I ask.

"We need to leave, now."

WE STAND IN LINE WITH THE CROWD OF PEOPLE WAITING TO enter. There's an empty pit in my stomach and my head aches. I have to do something. What's the point of being other and special if I can't help my friends? By doing what though? What can I do, without pulling the full attention of a mega-bunker down on me? A mega-bunker with at least two Dragons at the head of it?

The line moves impossibly slow. Nervously I ring my

hands, eyes darting from place to place. Silas places his hands on mine and gives me a look. He's right, we're on display and they're all watching, competing and searching for signs of weakness. Anything they can use or exploit to their own personal benefit. Taking a deep breath, I draw on reserves I'm not sure I have, forcing myself to find control.

If nothing else Silas has taught me that. There's a low buzz of conversation as people discuss which way they're going to bet, the specials or the monsters. Waves of nausea pass over me. Someone says it's a fight to the death and my head spins. Tightening my grip on Silas' arm I steady myself.

To the death. My friend's death. My guardian's death. Well lady, that's not gonna happen, not while I draw breath. Steeling my resolve, I focus and exert absolute control over myself. I will do whatever it takes to save them.

It's not much longer before we're in the room along with hundreds of the wealthy and well-to-do. There's so much money on display that directly juxtaposes the life I know the rest of the world is living and it makes me ill. It's not right. They're betting and laughing and carrying on when the lives of my friends are at stake. This is the value they put on the lives of others. The absolute disregard and display of care-lessness is shocking. If you're not one of them, you're worthless.

The middle of the room is dominated by a massive cage made of thick Nusteel bars. It's clear that whatever is going to be fighting in there, they want to make sure it doesn't escape. Which doesn't bode well for my friends.

Breathe, Aviella, I remind myself. Focus. There's too many eyes on me.

Risers are set up around the cage with rows of over-stuffed chairs. Everything is arranged to make sure that everybody has a good view of the fights. Silas guides me towards a set of seats. Eyes are on us, watching, and judging everything. There's as much danger out here as there will be inside that cage.

A man walks into the center of the cage and a hush falls over the crowd as everyone's attention focuses on him. He stands quietly drinking it in, reveling in it. I feel him feeding on it somehow, drawing their adoration in like its sustenance. He turns a slow circle, holding his arms out to either side, his gaze sweeping over the crowd. His suit is covered in rhinestones that catch the light and sparkle as he turns.

"Ladies and gentlemen," he says, and somehow his voice reaches every person in the room without him having to yell. "We have a special treat for your entertainment this evening. An angel! A demon! There is no way these two should ever meet as allies but in this strange and twisting world in which we live, anything is possible. Prepare yourselves and get your bets placed. They will be tested, and you will be entertained."

The crowd applauds and cheers. He bows then straightens and walks to a small door in the side of the cage where a guard opens the door and lets him out. When he shuts the gate it clangs loudly with an echo of finality.

Inside the cage another gate rattles as it lifts. Rafe and Nathaniel walk out of a tunnel. They're armed with steel swords and shields but also shirtless, with no armor or protection. They walk to the middle of the cage and stand back to back, ready for battle. There's an air of calmness about them like they don't have a care in the world. My heart pounds in my chest. They'll be okay. They have to be. If not… Silas tightens his grip on my hand, it's reassuring.

A bell rings and silence falls over the room. Another gate rattles open and a massive undead thing that looks like five professional wrestlers were melded into one giant, ugly monstrosity stumbles out. Nathaniel and Rafe turn and face it.

"You have to get them out of there," I hiss.

The person sitting beside me casts a sidelong glance. Dammit, I'm attracting attention. Silas shakes his head, almost imperceptibly. I tighten my grip on his arm, digging my fingernails in and clench my teeth as I try to keep my cool.

The undead thing stumbles forward, swinging its massive tree trunk-like arms at Rafe. My demon moves like lightning. Holding the thing's attention, dodging in and out and stabbing it with his sword. Nathaniel stares at the creature and chants in an ancient tongue, causing the monster to slow, but not stop. It's enough for Rafe and moments later he has sliced the thing into a dozen pieces that are lying scattered across the ground.

The crowd boos. It's a soft, controlled boo, nothing too rowdy for this group. Cutting through their displeasure is a single clap. It's loud and demanding of attention. Looking around for the source, I find it at the far end of the cage. Sitting on a raised dais are chairs that could rightly be called thrones. Alaric and Shen sit there, lording over the fights with the strength of their presence alone. Shen is clapping, slowly bringing his hands together and in a moment the crowd follows suit. Alaric is staring directly at me with a half-smile fixed on his face. His copper eyes dance with some infernal delight that makes my blood boil.

Rafe bows to the crowd. Nathaniel moves next to him, standing stoic and ready. The gate rattles open again, and another creature enters the cage. My boys turn back to the fight.

There doesn't seem to be an end to the number of monstrosities that they have to send at them. One after another, creatures are released into the cage with barely a moment to rest between them. It's clear they're not going to stop until Rafe and Nathaniel are dead. My boys have beaten six creatures so far but each new one is bigger and badder than the last.

Rafe has long gashes down his left side where he failed to dodge the claws of the last thing they fought. Their energy is wavering. I will them more, trying to pour energy into them through the connection between us, but it doesn't seem to be having any effect.

Cold sweat breaks out across me as another creature enters the arena. It looks like a giant bat with a scorpion's tail and razor-sharp claws along the edges of its leathery wings. Nathaniel and Rafe exchange a glance. Rafe shakes his head and sighs and the crowd perks up, sensing weakness.

The bat-like thing screeches, setting my nerves on edge. It leaps up, spreading its leathery wings. Either they aren't big enough to let the creature fly or there's not enough room in the cage, either way it doesn't get airborne, it can only lunge. Rafe rushes it, obviously trying to end the battle fast while Nathaniel dodges to the side. The creature screams and swings its tail, catching Nathaniel. He flies through the air and slams against the cage with a sickening thump. I can't stop a gasp before it escapes my mouth.

Nathaniel slides down the bars, crumpling to the ground like a broken toy. Rafe fights bravely, darting in and out, stabbing when he can but he's too busy trying dodging the tail and the claws. He's barely landing any blows.

Nathaniel struggles to his feet, shaking his head, a trail of blood drips down his chin from his mouth and nose. My heart pounds in my chest and my power thrums through my blood. I have to help them. Silas looks at me, silently urging me to remain discrete.

Pushing it down, I try to put my trust in the boys' abilities. Nathaniel steps forward at the same time that Rafe ducks under the swinging tail. I think for a moment it's about to turn in their favor but then everything goes wrong.

The creature screams, opening wide, revealing row after row of razor sharp teeth. It swings its wings in and slams into both of my men. They fly backwards, slamming against the cage. The Nusteel bars rattle with the force of their hit.

The creature's tail raises up over its back to strike, swinging forward. They boys aren't moving. One of them is going to die.

Fury explodes, I must stop this. Now

"No!" I scream.

Power rips out and down into the stone floor beneath my feet. The room rumbles then shakes. The floor cracks at my feet and a chasm races from me towards the creature. It looks around, screeching as the ground opens underneath and it falls. Rafe and Nathaniel grab the bars of the cage to avoid a similar fate.

"I told you to stay hidden," Silas hisses.

Everyone in the room is staring, they all know I did it. The hairs on back of my neck rise and my cheeks flush hot with anger. It doesn't matter, I had to save Rafe and Nathaniel. The moment breaks as screams cut through the air and chaos erupts. Guards rush into the crowd as it pushes towards the exits. Confusion reigns.

The cage is damaged, broken open where the rift runs through it. Climbing around knocked over chairs, I force my way past the screaming bodies towards it. Silas grabs my arm and pulls me back.

"We have to save them," I shout, turning on him.

"There's no time," he yells.

I jerk my arm free of his, glaring at him. "Then I'll make time," I say, spinning on my heel.

People push towards me with terror on their faces. Flashbacks of when the Seals were breaking dance through my thoughts as I try to fight my way through. Silas curses but I don't bother seeing if he's following.

The crowd surges, pushing me back and I'm swept along with them. My power buzzes in my bones, energy rising as my frustration mounts. Struggling to not let it slip out, I fight my way forward and I almost contain it but someone slams into me with an elbow to the head. Pain blooms blindingly bright.

That's all it takes. My power explodes and the crowd parts around me, cowering backwards. A circle clears around me and I'm alone and exposed. Mouths agape they stare at me. I'm not sure what I've done but their fear is obvious. Behind the ring of cowering people, I lock eyes with Shen and Alaric. They watch with knowing smiles on their faces. Cold chills run through my limbs and my stomach sinks through the floor.

Crap.

Something dances in their eyes, deep and undeniably dark. Shen arches an eyebrow and something in me responds as if he's calling me. Involuntarily, I take a step towards him, like my body isn't under my control.

"We have to go, now," Silas says, grabbing my arm in a tight grip.

He glances at the Dragons before spinning me around and breaking their hold on me. I stumble gasping for air. I've never felt anything like that. What did they do? How did they--?

Cold chills run down my spine and I know we have to get out of here before they get close to me again.

"What about—"

"I'll figure something out," he answers before I can finish, pulling me through the crowd.

Damn it, I've made another big mess. Fear and fury war as we make our way through a hidden side door.

~

Silas pauses and looks back before he slams the library door closed.

"I told you how important it was to remain hidden," he snaps.

"I couldn't just do nothing!"

Silas is jamming books into a bag. He looks up with a hard stare and I meet his gaze, unflinching. If I hadn't acted Rafe and Nathaniel would be dead. I won't allow that.

"We have to get you out of here, now," he says. "The Dragons are circling."

"Where am I going to go?"

Silas pauses, staring at the bag in his hand. When he looks up there's a weariness to him and his aura, a weight far beyond anything a human age should bring. "There's a rebellion here," he says. "They've built something of a city beneath the city."

"What about Rafe? Nathaniel? And Efram?"

Silas doesn't look up from packing as he shakes his head. I want to argue with him, pry, but I know him too well. We spent quite a bit of time in my studies and when he goes silent like this, there's no getting him to talk. Resignation fills me, and I make my decision. I'll go with him, for now, but I won't leave this bunker without my friends.

Decision made, I jump in and help with the packing. He's mostly concerned with grabbing books he thinks I'll need for my studies. Once we have all of those we're ready. Silas leads us through the stacks of books to a blank wall. He glances side to side as if making sure no one is watching, even though we're alone. Apparently satisfied he places a hand on the wall and his energy surges. My own power throbs in time with his as the wall swings open, revealing a hidden tunnel. He stands to one side and motions me inside. Looking back over my shoulder I cast a final glance over the library.

I haven't known a home since I left the orphanage. I

thought perhaps this library would be it. It's not to be, and the worst part of it all is it's my fault. I screw it up every time. I have to learn to control this power within me. I can't keep calling attention down on myself. Memories of Bunker E247 come unbidden and bile rises in my throat. I must do better, for everyone's sake.

Following Silas through the dark tunnels I note that, unlike every other part of Bunker 2, these have no cameras. He remains tightlipped and silent. I don't have anything to say either. Everything feels heavy, weighted with the knowledge that it's all my fault.

We come to another blank wall which Silas opens with his magic and we step out into a rough-cut tunnel. I glance around and notice this one also has no cameras and doesn't seem to be very well-traveled. He makes a quick glance around then heads off to the right. It's not long before we come to a massive iron door. Silas passes a hand over it and sigils glow. He grabs the handle, twists and the door swings open with a screech.

Standing on the other side of the door is Efram, grinning from ear to ear. My heart leaps into my throat.

"You can't get rid of me that easy," he smiles.

I squeal and jump to him, not caring who's watching as I wrap my arms around him. He returns my embrace, pulling me tight against him. I'm so excited I can't speak.

"She can't stay here," Silas says, interrupting our reunion.

Efram releases me, holding me at arm's length and looking me up and down.

"You look good," he says, before turning his attention to Silas. "I heard about the tournament."

"Have you heard anything about Rafe and Nathaniel?" I interrupt.

Efram nods, not taking his attention off Silas.

"We will all need clearance," Efram says. "We're not going to send her off on her own."

"Yes, we do," Silas agrees.

"What are you guys talking about? How do we get Rafe and Nathaniel out of the cages?" I ask. "There's no way I'm leaving them behind."

"We have friends here," Silas says, cryptic as usual. "Keep her safe until I get back."

"Got it," Efram says.

Silas heads off and Efram takes my hand. leading me through the new tunnels. He takes us to a small bunk room, not nearly as nice as he had before, but there are shelves and shelves full of expensive looking baubles.

Efram starts packing his things and I pass the time looking them over. Most of them seem frivolous. The kind of things that only the wealthy would bother with having, no functional purpose that I can see.

"Where did you get all this stuff?"

"Gifts," he says, not stopping what he's doing.

"Gifts?" I ask, a jealous twinge twists my heart.

"Uh-huh."

"Gifts from who?"

What is wrong with me? Why do I care where he got these things?

"Clients," he says.

"Women?"

"Mostly," he says, pausing in his work.

The burning in my blood reaches my cheeks and my chest tightens. "A lot of women?" I ask, not sure I want to know the answer.

He looks at me and I catch a flash of humor in his eyes.

"None that hold a candle to you, love. I was bored out of my mind," he says.

Love? The tightness in my chest releases and I can't help smiling.

"You're too cheesy," I say and he grins.

He called me love. My cheeks burn hot.

Silas walks into the room, breaking any moment that might have been between Efram and I. He looks serious, as usual, his eyes scanning, taking it all in.

"Come with me," he says. "Bring all your things."

He leads us out into the tunnels and we emerge into a main corridor where are the stalls of a fully functioning marketplace, armed security teams, and people going about their daily lives. It really is a city of its own. Try as I might to locate them, I don't spot any cameras. That is completely different than Bunker 2 above us.

Following Silas through the marketplace, no one seems to pay us any attention. Silas leads the way to a main building then into an office space. Inside are a well-dressed man and a woman who have the air of being in charge.

"Any news?" Silas asks, without preamble.

"Your packages are being transported to the intensive infirmary," the man says.

"They'll conveniently be lost in transport," the woman adds.

Silas nods. "Good."

"We've arranged chambers for you while we work on transportation," the man says.

I watch, feeling out of place. No one is paying attention to Efram or I. It's as if we don't matter or don't exist. My worry and questions burn in me, demanding answers.

"What does that mean?" I ask. "Are you talking about Rafe and Nathaniel? Are they going to be okay?"

The man and the woman and Silas look at me. I've got that sensation of being put on the spot and knowing I've spoken when I shouldn't have, but I don't care. I'm worried about my friends and I want answers.

"Aviella," Silas says, his voice sonorous.

"Don't Aviella me," I say, putting my foot down. "I want to know they're okay. That's not too much to ask."

"It's not too much to ask that you keep your powers under control either," the man says.

"Avoiding the attention of the Dragons would've been better for everyone," the woman says.

"Yeah, I got it. I know what I did. Who are you and are my friends okay?" I demand, pushing past their arguments.

The man and the woman exchange a look. Efram places his hand on my arm and he pushes calming energy into me, but I shake it off. I'm too irritated to be pacified. I want some damn answers.

"Aviella," Efram says, feeling my resistance. "These are the leaders of the resistance. They're going to help us get out of here."

"Okay, thank you," I say, only partially satisfied. "What about Nathaniel and Rafe?"

"They will be safe," the man says. "Give us some time."

Great. Time, the one thing I never feel I have enough of.

"All right," I say, resigning myself to it, then as an after-thought I add, "I do appreciate it."

We're taken to the chambers they offered. Each of us has a bunk space of our own that, compared to what I'm used to, is quite luxurious. Not so much in furnishings but just the fact of having a private, quiet space to be in. I sit down on the bed and realize I'm exhausted. Lying down I let my spinning thoughts carry me into sleep.

Efram called me love.

" $\mathcal{A}$ viella, wake up," Efram says.
I jerk awake and sit up straight. Blinking sleep from my eyes I try to focus.

"What—"

"They've arrived," Efram says. "They're going to be okay."

There's no need for him to say who he means. My heart soars as I leap to my feet.

"Oh, thank you," I say, wrapping my arms around him.

Our bodies meld together and he feels so right being this close. I linger in his arms, enjoying the moment. His energy melds with mine and I feel his enjoyment of the moment too.

"Come on, I'll take you to them," he says, stepping back.

Holding my hand, he leads me to a compartment with two guards outside the door who nod as we walk through.

"I don't need your help," Rafe complains. "See to Nathaniel, he's worse off than I am."

Pushing past Efram, I rush into the room. Two people are trying to force Rafe onto a table with healing lights but he's resisting. Nathaniel is being assisted by another person to lay down on a separate table.

"Maybe you should be a little bit less stubborn," I say.

"Aviella!" Rafe exclaims.

He tries to push past the two orderlies but when he does, one of their arms brushes against his ribs and he yelps in pain.

"Okay, okay," Rafe agrees, giving in.

"Exactly," I say, smiling so wide it hurts my mouth.

It's so good to see them. Nathaniel looks at me and smiles and then closes his eyes as the orderlies turn the medical lights on. Rafe decides to comply, lying down on the medical bed himself.

"I wanted to make sure you were okay," Rafe says.

"I'm fine," I say. "It's so good to see you."

"Of course it is, I'm awesome," the demon jokes.

"I'm glad you're okay," Nathaniel says, his tone reserved as always.

"It's good to see you too," I say to him.

I'm certain I see a smile flutters across his lips.

"Okay, we should let them heal," Efram says.

"Sure," I agree. "Rafe be nice. I won't be far away."

"Me? I'm always nice," he says.

I step out with Efram and he closes the door behind us.

"Nathaniel will be out for at least a week. Rafe will probably be down a day at most, demons on his level heal pretty quickly," Efram says. "We'll all be fine. Next, we're going to get out of here, hopefully before the Dragons find us."

An overwhelming sense of happiness wells up. Everything is working out better than I could've hoped. Efram is so close, his presence engulfs me. I lean into his solid body, looking up into his eyes. He leans closer and my breath catches, certain this is it. Anticipation coils like a tightrope in my center.

Dammit Efram. Get with it!

Rising onto my toes I claim his lips, stealing the kiss I

know he wants to give. He stiffens for an instant and then our energies meld together and he gives in, grasping the hair at the back of my head in a firm grip and claiming my mouth with his own. It's everything I've ever imagined. His tongue licks across my lips and invades my mouth with crushing force.

His strong arms pull me tight against him. Our energies spinning together carries me up and away, making me lighter. For once, everything in the world is right.

He pulls back from the kiss, our lips lingering together.

"We should be careful of distraction until we are on firmer ground, love," he breathes against my mouth.

As much as I want to argue, I know the truth of his words. We're in danger here. The Dragons are looking for me, the shadow powers are looking for me, and destiny definitely isn't through with me yet.

Holding my hand, he leads the way back to our compartments. Going through the marketplace and looking around at the sea of faces, dirty and hopeless, I spot Silas. He's moving among the downtrodden, handing out food from a bag at his side.

The rings of destiny tighten around me. For the first time in my life, I think I'm exactly where I'm supposed to be. I'm on the path that I'm supposed to follow. I don't know how I know, but I do. It's a truth that resonates deep in my bones. At least now, unlike before, I won't face it alone.

Continue *the Power of Twelve* series in book two,
**Apocalypse the Blossoming**.

SUBSCRIBE TO MIRANDA MARTIN'S MAILING LIST
Are you interested in getting the latest updates from Miranda Martin? You'll be automatically welcomed with the subscriber exclusive *Alien Prince*. Once or twice a month, Miranda sends out sneak peeks of works in progress, shiny new covers, hot deals and sales, giveaways and more!

mirandamartinromance.com
miranda@mirandamartinromance.com

# ABOUT THE AUTHOR

USA Today Bestselling Author of fantasy and scifi romance, Miranda Martin's books feature larger than life heroes with out-of-this-world anatomy and smart heroines destined to save the world. As a little girl she would sneak off with her nose in a book, dreaming of magical realms. Today she brings those fantasies to life and adores every fan who chooses to live in them for a while.

She was born and raised in southern Virginia, but as a veteran she's traveled to places like Korea, Hawaii and good 'ole Texas. Now she's settled in Kansas, the heart of America, with her husband and daughters. Her favorite animals are dragons, unicorns, and cats. If she's not writing, you can still find her tucked away somewhere with a warm blanket and her nose in a book.

*Get in touch!*
mirandamartinromance.com
miranda@mirandamartinromance.com

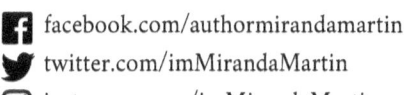

facebook.com/authormirandamartin
twitter.com/imMirandaMartin
instagram.com/imMirandaMartin

www.ingramcontent.com/pod-product-compliance
Lightning Source LLC
Chambersburg PA
CBHW031219260626
47169CB00007B/2114